THE DREADFUL DOCTOR FAUST COLLECTION

THE DREADFUL DOCTOR FAUST COLLECTION

K.H. KOEHLER

The Monster Factory

CONTENTS

| 1 | Foreword by Michele Lee | 1 |

THE DREADFUL DOCTOR FAUST

2	Then	4
3	Now	6
4	Then	16
5	Now	26
6	Then	38
7	Now	53
8	Then	70

| 9 | Now | 82 |

BRIDE OF DOCTOR FAUST

10	Below	96
11	Above	108
12	Below	132
13	Above	143
14	Below	150
15	Above	159
16	Below	164
17	Above	167
18	Below	177
19	Above	180

FOR THE ONE I LOVE: A DOCTOR FAUST STORY

20 February 14, 20--   200

ABOUT THE AUTHOR

Copyright © 2018 by K.H. Koehler

All rights reserved. No part of this publication may be reproduced, stored or transmitted in any form or by any means, electronic, mechanical, photocopying, recording, scanning, or otherwise without written permission from the publisher. It is illegal to copy this book, post it to a website, or distribute it by any other means without permission.

This novel is entirely a work of fiction. The names, characters and incidents portrayed in it are the work of the author's imagination. Any resemblance to actual persons, living or dead, events or localities is entirely coincidental.

Paperback ISBN: 979-8-8692-2804-8

Ebook ISBN: 979-8-8692-2805-5

Cover art and interior design by KH Koehler Design

https://khkoehler.net

No part of this book was created using artificial intelligence.

| 1 |

Foreword by Michele Lee

Literature has long been allowed to, even obligated to, explore ideas, places, and people that make readers uncomfortable. Horror is best known for confronting the more physical ideas that discomfort us. Whether it's a *femme fatale* who means us harm, the random attention of a serial killer or monster who promises us pain and death, or the simple physical terror of our bodies failing or rebelling against us, horror takes us through brutal places and reoccurring themes of physicality.

In this collection, readers will meet The Dreadful Dr. Faust and his Poppet, creatures separated from the human race through excruciating deaths, horrifying re-shapings, and bloody rebirths. Part *Frankenstein*, part *Dracula*, and part Jack the Ripper. Dr. Faust and his love heal the sick, save the desperate, protect the weak, and punish the evil. Koehler's twin tales are like beautifully-forged daggers, lovely, shiny to behold, but wicked-sharp and dangerous.

Straight out of gothic traditions, but with a modern sensibility that would make Victorian prudes blush, Koehler's Faust tales are a dark gem glimmering in all the blood, viscera, and torn flesh of today's horror genre. Enjoy the transformation.

~ Michele Lee, Author of *Wolf Heart* and *Rot*

THE DREADFUL DOCTOR FAUST

| 2 |

Then

The Church of Saint Bridget sat disemboweled.
Built in 1873 on the East River waterfront by the well-meaning Irish immigrants of Vinegar Hill, it failed to thrive despite their nurturing. Some said it was the dead brown fish smell of the river that wafted through the open clerestory windows in the summer, or the cobblestoned roads that never saw repair, or the careless rambling look of the cathedral, so at odds with the shapely modern white chapels that had come to dot Brooklyn. There may have been a history of violence or some mischief, but if so, the story had never come to light.

In only a hundred years, the church had become a shell. By the late 1970s, the last bits of statuary had been scraped from the structure in a thorough religious abortion, and the grounds de-sanctified. Time and blistering industrial wind did their work. The cathedral leaned, the unwelcomed light of day spiking through massive nesting holes in the ceiling. Mosaic windows, once full of leering Ecclesiastical images, were kicked out by kids so that jagged glass glinted like alien orifices all over the surface of the building. Inside, the crumbling plaster, studs, and buckled floor made a deathtrap for the children who dared each other to venture into the structure. There were tarry patches of oil upon which floated crushed beer cans, used condoms, syringes. The floor simmered with dust and rats.

Urban renewal was discussed, the church boarded over and yellow-taped for demolition, then abandoned when the investor lost his capital, his life savings, and eventually swallowed a bullet. Slopes of debris from demolished buildings to either side embraced the church. It was soon forgotten, protected by an urban wasteland of darkness, time, pollution.

Sometimes garbage floated down from the Long Island Sound and found itself tongued ashore by the East River running brown and relentless past the church. And sometimes a few mottled blue-black bodies turned up, as well, thrown off the Brooklyn Bridge like unwanted pets, eyes blind eggs in waxen faces so like mannequins. But the corpses didn't linger long among the debris; they were efficiently dragged off by the clans of scavenging dogs that lived around the church.

When the body of the girl drifted to shore among the other refuse, there was no one to see, and no dogs. It lay green and heavy like a marble statue left out in the rain. It did not move, except for the occasional shudder like a little orgasm of pain rippling through the fish-white flesh.

The man in black found the girl in the moments before daybreak. She was tall, insect-thin, with small, young apple-like breasts and long dancer's legs. Her hair was very long, and full of mildewing leaves like some siren coughed up out of the water in an old myth. She had been chewed, swallowed, and digested by the city. Now she was excrement. Like the church, expelled. She might have been pretty, once; he didn't know. The girl had no face, just a red gaping wound where a pretty face might once have been.

He lifted her quivering weight into his arms and carried her into the ruined corpse of the church, into that place of the dead.

| 3 |

Now

The girl with the long hair and mismatched eyes stepped through the doors of the academy just as the final class of the day was letting out. Girls flew past her, a blur of checked skirts and maroon vests over sweaty white button-down blouses. They were burning off the last energy of the day, rushing to practice, rehearsals, or club. They noticed the new girl for perhaps half a second, but so preoccupied were they, that few of them remembered her, even after all had come to pass.

The girls hated the uniforms, of course, trashing them in subtle ways. Fencenet stockings under knee-high socks, black lace bras peeking through skin-thin shirts. But the new girl's uniform was virgin, starched razor straight. She was tall and bony, like a young filly that still needed to grow into her skin. Her hair was long and jet-black and framed a sunless white face made all of dire planes, the homely beauty of a young British actress. Her eyes were hard, like crystal, and of two different colors. Sometimes they sent the problem girls from the Bronx down here on scholarships. Good Works, they called it.

It wasn't unusual for new faces to crop up unexpectedly.

And so, as the students fled en masse toward their destinations, no one felt concerned.

By the following day, the girl had disappeared. And in many ways, she had never been there at all.

* * *

Jerry Pacino was dying for a smoke.

He guided the heavy, chalk-dusted broom down the central hallway of the academy. Twenty-two years of picking up after the brats, and he had cleaned up every imaginable substance, and a few he'd rather not think about. He let it clack to the floor and lit up, gravitating toward one of the closed classrooms.

The lights were off and the room was dim, but not dark. He went to the bank of windows and cranked a pane out to air the room as he smoked. Over twenty years, and what had he to show for it but calluses, a nagging cough, and this bank of windows that showed whiteness in winter, green in spring, and the crisp red and fawn colors of autumn.

He peered out at the dark shadows amassing on the soccer field—girls kicking a ball through the wheat-colored grass, screaming, the setting sun making them featureless black ghosts. There was a chill under his limp blue uniform, a kind of unfathomable fatigue that felt too much like despair. He coughed it up to the insomnia; he hadn't slept right in months, not since that crazy bitch came slamming against his door in the middle of the night, waking him and Nora from a sound sleep.

But this was New York. The city was full of crackheads. The couple downstairs had wild rows every night that rattled the eighty-year-old plumbing. And, once, upstairs, some kid passed out over his pipe and left his faucet on all night. The water managed to cave in part of the ceiling over the kitchen. It was months before the landlord repaired it, and there were still dings in Nora's kettle from the accident.

Then there was that time—ten years ago if he remembered right—when Nora took in a runaway who stole five hundred dollars from her. Never again. Jerry told her. And Jerry had stayed true to his promise, even that night when Nora climbed out of bed in her hairnet and diabetic socks and said the girl at their door sounded like she was in trouble.

"Remember what happened with that bitch?" Jerry roared softly into the pillow under his chin.

"I know, Jer, but..."

"Forgetaboutit. Call the police."

Nora did. But by the time the uniforms arrived, the frenetic pounding had subsided. Jerry told them some wild party was going on next door, kids out of control, some girl high as a kite on smack, from the sound of her—or whatever they were smoking these days.

But the investigating cops found no girl. No party. It was surreal, an annoyance.

Nora wouldn't let it go. She nagged him until it was all he could do to get out in the morning.

A few days later, Jerry stepped out into the hall, picked up his neighbor's mail, and knocked on his door. When the young man answered—Tim, his name was, if Jerry wasn't mistaken—Jerry handed over a cable bill, telling him it had gotten mixed in with Jerry's own mail.

Tim wasn't at all like the brats he cleaned up after. Groomed, shy, with amazing black philosopher's eyes. His apartment was spotless and landscaped with old Chippendale furniture and throw afghans. Dusty light slivered through the chintzy curtains and spotlighted old family pictures, frayed leather-bound books, benign knickknacks. Jerry commented on how similar their apartments were, even down to the "bric-a-brac" (Nora's word for stuff). The boy smiled and said it was his mother's.

Nora had wanted Jerry to ask about the girl, but wild girls like that weren't the kind of dates that young men like Tim brought home to meet their mothers. Jerry went back inside and forgot about the incident, except at night, when he dreamed.

Jerry tossed the cigarette out the open window. He had just one room left to do.

Generally speaking, he disliked the school auditorium. After hours it was tragically unlit, the flags on the walls amorphous squares of darkness, the arched windows—for the room doubled as a chapel—bleeding in watery colored light that never quite reached the aisles between chairs. Tonight there was only one dim light burning high above the stage, shining down on the background scenery of an Austrian mountainside, painted by the art class in long slopes of green and brown for the school production of *The Sound of Music*.

The pneumatic door slowly hissed closed behind him as he pushed his bulk through. Otherwise, the place was as soundless as a tomb.

He started down the aisle, his janitor's bucket thrust out before him like a lance. He was alone and the place was deathly quiet, yet a part of him quivered within.

He thought the place was empty until he noticed the body of the girl lying prone on the stage. "Hey," said Jerry. His unkempt smoker's voice cut into the deafening silence like an unwelcomed knife. He was irritated. But he wasn't afraid, not then, and not until the very end.

If this was the brats' idea of a joke...

In twelve strides, he was down the aisle. In six, he was at the top of the stage. That was when he felt the first twinge of real concern.

The girl was lying in a dramatic posture on the stage, arms outflung, legs bent at the knees as if she had been crucified. Her face was turned on a sea of hair like frayed black silk.

"Hey," Jerry said again, hovering uselessly. "Hey, are you all right?"

The girl opened her eyes. Her face was milk-white, her eyes queer, one a pale watery blue, the other a deep Asian black. Instead of answering him, the girl with the eyes slowly pulled herself upright with the paralyzing grace of a pole dancer.

She stood there as if listening for a cue. Then, like something carefully choreographed, she extended her arms longingly to the darkness beyond the stage curtain. Moments later, she was joined by a man, tall and slim, and outfitted entirely in black.

Jerry felt his reality shift half a foot to the left. The man was dressed in a dark stiff suit, a standing collar, and a solitaire, like something from an old British cozy. A wide-brimmed black felt hat slanted across the face, hiding much of it from view, but from what Jerry could tell, the man was ghastly white beneath.

With a flourish, he reached for the girl, pantomiming concern, his shining, black-gloved hands closing about her delicate wrists. With exaggerated care, he waltzed her across the stage like Fred Astaire and Ginger Rogers high-stepping past a muzzy late-night TV screen. Jerry watched him slant her slight figure into the circle of his arms. The girl lolled back in her partner's embrace in a kind of slow-motion *ballet d'action*. Exquisite, dreamlike. Part of the play?

Then Jerry saw again the backdrop of green and golden Salzburg Mountains. There was no scene like this in the play. He knew that. *The Sound of Music* was a favorite of Nora's.

Jerry tried to laugh off the absurdity of the performance, but the man in the antique clothes turned his partner in a pirouette and the girl jumped like a stringless marionette. There was a flash-like light through the colored windows.

Jerry felt no pain, but a gush of flowering red hit the white face of the man in black. It gusted over the girl, over her horsey, pale, unpretty face. Beads of blood clung to her long, curling lashes and were blinked away like red tears.

Jerry slid, soundless, to the floor of the stage, in his mind protecting his throat even as his conscious thought began ebbing away with his blood. The girl who had cut his throat was frozen in place like a sculpture. He looked and he saw the exquisite glint of the surgeon's scalpel in her upraised hand, a blade dipped in bright red paint. He saw the depthless shine of her unblinking eyes. She looked as pleased with herself as Sweeney Todd about to break out in song.

These brats, he thought.

Darkness swallowed him up for some time.

* * *

Jerry opened his eyes to a pale, smeary darkness.

It was dim, but he picked out little details. Distant tiled walls, a numbing silence, the disconcerting shine of stainless steel so suggestive of hospitals and morgues.

For many hours, he had floated inside a warm sea of drug-induced half-dreams. Many times, he had tried to call out, but all he could manage was a pained moan. He slept and woke and slept again on the undulating waves of glistening unconsciousness.

But this time he didn't sleep. This time he was aware.

Something important must have occurred. A fall. Or his heart. He hoped it wasn't his heart. He glanced around, searching for Nora, expecting to find her seated beside his bed in a deathwatch, but he found he was alone.

He was so dry, his tongue moving like a fat worm in his mouth. He wanted to summon a nurse, but his body felt like lead. He could not even lift his arms.

Somewhere in the swimmy darkness, a door opened, and bright artificial lights flicked on. Now he saw the room in clear detail, the painful white sterility of a vast operation theatre. It felt as cold as an alien ship.

A man and a woman stood over him.

Jerry had to shuffle the images in his brain before he placed them. The man wore black and had no face...no, his face wasn't absent, only masked in frightening bandages, with small slits for the eyes and mouth, with tiny shards of mirror-like eyes glinting out. The woman, though, worried him more. She was beautiful and ugly all at once, and awash in great reams of black satin hair. He knew them both...but from where?

"Welcome back, Mr. Pacino," said the man in black. His voice was a brimming dark baritone with a vibrating British inflection, muffled but not softened by the bandages. "I trust you are comfortable? That you slept well?"

The sight of the pair of them made a trill of danger sound down Jerry's back. He tried to speak, but he had no voice, just a bee-like burr of noise in his throat.

"Please do not strain yourself," the man in black said thoughtfully. "You are still healing." He inclined his head in greeting. "I am the Doctor." Then he glanced aside at the woman. "And this is my assistant, Poppet."

The Doctor cut such a powerfully strange figure, Jerry didn't notice until that moment that the woman he called Poppet was dressed like a Gibson girl in a long dress of shining jet black moiré with puffed sleeves and a bustled waist. What a strange girl, he thought.

Then he recognized the mismatched eyes. He remembered. Instinct made him want to shift away from the girl, to protect his throat from her knife, but his arms refused to work.

"I believe Mr. Pacino is prepared to join the others in the Gallery now," said the Doctor to his assistant. "Bring him, Poppet, won't you?"

Wordlessly, she wheeled him from the operation theatre and down a long corridor that stretched into darkness and dripping cold. The walls were not white tile, as Jerry had expected, but of some porous concrete that the chill and moisture clung to like sweat. There were old iron-banded doors on both sides, like something from a medieval dungeon. Pipes ran down the length of the corridor, dripping down noxious wetness onto Jerry's face. And from all around came distant murmuring high notes that might have been human voices crying out from the depths of some undiscovered Hell.

What is this place? He wondered. Long before they reached his cell, the terror solidified into something hard and bitter and spoiled within him.

The Doctor held a door open. He seemed to sense his patient's distress. "I have given you a great gift, Mr. Pacino," he said as they maneuvered Jerry's gurney into the room. "Life everlasting—more than any god has ever granted mortal human flesh. Like Hercules, you have labored and will now exist immemorial."

The words made no sense to Jerry.

The cell was small and windowless and of that curious dripping grey concrete, a desolate hole in the ground. Jerry breathed in the dirty air and began to struggle in earnest, finally dislodging the sheet covering him. He wanted to grab and tear at the two of them, kick at them, these pious evil performers in their fancy dress and stage eyes, but he found himself quite unable to move. He had no arms, no legs, though streaks of phantom pain radiated from the centermost part of his body outward.

The Doctor turned to leave with Poppet. "Welcome to the Gallery, Mr. Pacino," he said. "Please enjoy your stay."

He left the room. He locked it behind him.

Alone, Jerry screamed soundlessly.

***

Years passed. And the Doctor's prophecy was fulfilled.

Jerry did not die. Indeed, after some time, he realized that it might not even be possible.

He saw the Doctor infrequently, a few times a year, and only on those long, unfortunate nights when the creature came harvesting flesh from what he called his "body farm," of which Jerry was an important part.

But even so, even were it possible to think through such harrowing pain, it was impossible to ask his benefactor any questions. Jerry's voice, like his arms and legs, was long gone, torn away like the material the Doctor sometimes took from him, material that grew back relentlessly, insolently.

Yet questions remained. Who was the Doctor? What power did he wield so flippantly? And what part did the Poppet play?

Most of all, why him?

The first long year was the worst. Jerry often thought about the girl in the Gibson dress, the one who had slit his throat. There was little else to ruminate on, to experience, in this deathless burial. But after a while, time itself lost its cloying effect. After a hundred years, Jerry ceased to recall the girl, or much about life beyond his tomb and the occasional, agonizing visits by the Doctor. He had no visitors except for the Doctor. He saw nothing but grey walls and his own empty thoughts imprinted on them.

One day he entertained the idea that he had always been a part of the Doctor's body farm. An extension, a dream.

And dreams do not ponder their realities.

* * *

Down in a small, inconsequential town in the middle of Kansas the mail didn't come around until after one in the afternoon, which was just fine with the old man. He had slept through the morning and well past noon. The phone had rung several times—his boss, he supposed—but he hadn't picked up.

He lay on greasy grey sheets that had not seen changing for the past four months and clutched a ragged stuffed monkey that had once belonged to his daughter. It was so old a button-eye was missing, and the stuffing jutted, disemboweled, from one side of the body. Occasionally he scratched at his pubes and listened to the prairie wind hissing incessantly through the seams of the trailer. Hunger, headache, and the need to urinate finally forced him to his feet.

The trailer was old, cantankerous, an aluminum frying pan in summer, an icebox in winter. The hallway was full of cobwebs and crumbling plaster. He paid it no mind. In the kitchenette, he put a fire-blackened kettle on to heat, then stepped outside, wincing and barefoot, and walked down the long gravel drive to the mailbox.

There were fliers, plackets of coupons, invitations from credit card companies and local churches. But today, among it all, was a plain white envelope addressed to him with a New York City postal seal. He felt a dull shock that nearly brought him crumbling to his knees there on the bare gravel drive that even the weeds had shunned.

Clawing open the envelope, he read the typewritten letter inside with a rising and falling heart.

| 4 |

Then

The girl who came from the river awoke to darkness and to the eroding echo of water falling on stone.

She blinked her eyes, but the darkness was the same either way. Her last echoing thought had been of crushing, unbreathable pain, and a base desire to move away from it. It spiked fear in her body, even now. She sucked in a deep breath that tasted of antiseptic and linen and sat bolt upright, prepared to rip at her face and the frightening bandages blinding her face—

"Don't do that," commanded a voice out of the impenetrable darkness.

She listened to her own panicked breathing—in, out, in, out—and slowly turned her head to find the source of the voice.

"Do not," the voice spoke again, "disturb the bandages." And then, as if to make up for such sudden harshness: "You are still healing, my dear."

The voice was soft, yet hard, almost metallic in strength, and very deep. It resonated around the black chamber and reminded her of some old British black and white movie watched on a long-ago Saturday morning. For some inexplicable reason, she was not afraid. She could listen to a voice like that forever. The wielder of such a voice could recite pi and hold someone spellbound.

But her body trembled with fear even as her spirit was quelled by the sound of the voice. "Where am I?" Each syllable sucked the bitter cloth into her mouth, and she had to stop herself from panicking at the awful pressure of the bandages.

Bandages meant something terrible had happened, something she was unprepared to deal with...

"You are safe," said the voice unhurriedly from across the room. "You are safe here."

"Where is here?"

"Below."

She didn't know what that meant, if anything. "Am...am I a prisoner?"

A pause. "Yes."

"I don't want to be a prisoner."

"My dear, you have no choice."

"Why?" she said. "Why am I here?"

Why am I alive? She wanted to ask. Her most recent memories were of a carnivorous darkness ripping at her flesh, tearing it off the bone.

"I found you," answered the voice, with a touch of annoyance, "by the river. Washed up. I remade you. You belong to me. It's only fair, don't you agree?"

His words angered her. And anger was an old friend. "Fuck you," she said defiantly.

The man who spoke to her stood up. "You must articulate. You do not want to fuck me, Poppet. You want to hurt me. To hurt me in response to the man who hurt you. Articulate."

"Fuck you," she responded. "Fuck you and fuck you and fuck you!" she screamed hysterically through the bitter bandages.

"You're a stupid little bitch," said the man. He was standing over her.

She swung her clawed hand at him, to strike him.

He caught it. His hand was cold and immovable, like a machine. An army of men could not have broken his grip on her.

She quivered, waiting for the killing blow to fall.

"You are mine," said the man. The sound of his voice was scorching, like the grind of gears. "Forget the rest. Forget the rage. Forget the pain. And do not raise your hand to me again, Poppet. I gave you this hand"—his fingers closed incrementally tighter about her wrist until she groaned at his strength—"and I can take it off."

He let her go.

He left her to wallow in darkness and questions for a long time.

* * *

Slowly, as the panic lessened, the girl became aware of a world surrounding her.

Voices. Sounds of footsteps, feral life. People passed in distant corridors, speaking in hushed voices as if afraid to awaken something in this place...this Below. Sometimes she heard the man's voice. Sometimes it was a woman who spoke. Sometimes she heard nothing at all, though she sensed the man's presence brushing past her like the flit of old moth wings. Always she heard the despondent drip of water on stone.

She slept for great unfathomable swaths of time.

A woman saw to her meager needs. She would come into the chamber and put on a record. The music was old and moving, dire. Then she would attend to the girl, changing soiled clothing or bedding. Sometimes she bathed the girl like a child. The girl would have been utterly mortified, but she was too weak to move. Breathing itself was a labor.

The woman who cared for her spoke little, but when she did, her voice was scouring. She was an old woman, hands aged into claws. She was not bothered by even the vilest of tasks. She simply did what the man asked her to do.

The girl asked about the Below, and about the man who had imprisoned her.

"We call him the Doctor," said the woman. Her name, the girl discovered, was Mary. "He takes care of us. We, in turn, take care of him."

Mary's voice was diffident, except when she spoke of the Doctor. Then it changed. It came alive. Mary smelled of talc and lavender, but there was an undercurrent of rot on her breath. She did not always answer the girl's questions.

"Is he really a doctor?" asked the girl.

Mary dressed her in a new nightgown.

"Where are we? What is the Below?"

The record played out. Mary did not answer.

In time, she left the room.

* * *

Time passed.

The girl's sleep grew lighter, discomforting. Her muscles cramped, wanting to move.

One day she climbed, swaying, to her feet, clinging to a bedpost to keep herself upright. She felt like a rag doll all pieced together.

She thought about the Doctor, what he said. I remade you. Whatever that meant.

She took her first faltering step like an infant and fell violently against the side of the bed, clutching at the bedclothes. The second step was easier, but she could not find her balance at all. It was like swimming in a dark ocean, where any direction might be up.

Mary came into the room and put her back to bed without aplomb.

"Let me go," she said to Mary through a slit in the bandages. Mary had cut one so she could take soup and water. The Doctor had ceased feeding her intravenously the day before.

Mary said, "The Doctor will soon return."

The girl lay tiredly on the pillows, awash with questions.

There were cats. One jumped all over the bed once Mary had left. The girl clutched it like a toy she had once loved and waited.

* * *

In the evenings, the Doctor visited her.

He fed her spoonfuls of a thin broth through the slit in the bandages. He did not hurt her again, or threaten her, though he did ask strange questions like, "What would you do if I kept you here forever, Poppet?" and "What if you were never allowed to leave?"

"I would find a way to escape," she answered simply.

"Would you, Poppet?" he answered. "And how would you go about accomplishing that task?"

"I don't know. I'd find a way." She thought a moment. "I would ask."

"And who would you ask?"

"You. I would ask you questions that would give me clues."

"Perhaps I would lie to mislead you. Perhaps I intend to kill you in time."

"You won't," she said.

"Why is that?"

"You aren't done hurting me yet." And the girl lowered her head.

* * *

Finally, the girl was able to walk the course of the room and all the way back to the bed before falling from exhaustion. But she did not tell the Doctor that when he visited her that evening.

Instead, she asked, "Who is Mary?"

The Doctor sat in the chair beside her bed. He had brought the evening's bowl of soup. One of the cats skittered by over the coverlet. "She is my assistant," he answered.

"Is she your wife?" the girl asked between spoonfuls of the soup.

"No."

She felt stronger, bolder. As he fed her, she reached out and touched the hand holding the spoon. She was surprised to find the Doctor's hand young, firm, cool. He wore rings.

The Doctor grew very still.

"Don't you like women?" the girl asked.

The Doctor was silent for a long moment. Then he said, "Women and I have grown apart."

"Why?"

He hesitated. "There has been too much time."

"Are you very old?"

"You talk like an ignorant child."

She swallowed. Waited.

He was invisible to her senses.

She said, "I'm not a child. I'm sixteen." One of the cats came up under her hand. She clutched it like a shield. "But I feel much older. Thirty-five. Forty."

"One day you will be," answered the Doctor. "One day you will be a hundred. Two hundred."

She laughed at his funny joke.

"You're a child," he said. "A poppet. Just that. Perhaps I should plait your hair. Dress you in a pinafore."

"Fuck you," she said, quietly, with subdued anger. "I'm not your doll."

"I should wash your mouth out with soap, Poppet."

"My name is Louise, not Poppet," she shouted.

He dropped the spoon into the soup. "Not anymore."

* * *

Eventually, Louise climbed out of bed and did not fall. She ached, but she could manage. Pain was an old ally.

She moved around the room, bumping into big pieces of furniture. There was a long dressing table with toiletries, a brush and a comb. Scissors. A trill of fear went up her back, but her hands were as steady as those of a surgeon as she cut through the bandages along the back of her head. Her hair spilled forth, damp and oily. The bandages came off like a mask imprinted with a human face.

Gaslight turned the antique bedchamber around her golden. It looked less like a bedroom and more like the burial tomb of an Egyptian pharaoh.

Louise felt nauseous. She dropped the mask of bandages at her feet. There was a round gilded mirror on the wall just above the dressing table. But her sight was dark and seemed to sleep within her. She stared into it until blurs became smudges and smudges slowly took the form of images.

She expected a monstrous face of ruined girlflesh. She was not prepared for the stranger's face looking back at her.

This girl looked older than she. Her face was swollen and discolored a bruised purple. But the flesh was whole. There was no monster, just this stunningly alien face full of sloping planes and two new eyes not her own, one the color of ink mixed with rain, the other the deep brown-black of a girl of the Orient.

She was bandaged over most of her body. But a calm indifference of the face gave her courage. She went to work with the scissors, shedding the linen like a chrysalis. There were no scars, no horrors, as she had expected. Her confidence grew. She lifted her arms and stared at her bony wrists, her lightly muscled arms, her high white breasts with their deep rose points, the clean-shaven whiteness at her groin, her long, even, unmarred legs.

The Doctor stood in the room behind her. She never heard his coming. In that way, he was like the cats.

She saw him first reflected in the mirror.

He was amazingly tall, as she had suspected, and dressed entirely in black. The dim lamplight of the room slivered across an antique pocket watch and brass cufflinks. His clothes were ridiculously proper. She expected something gothic, but he was more like a talented young actor playing Professor Moriarty on television than a vampire exhumed from his crypt of a thousand years.

Only his face made her pause. It was masked in bandages as hers had been. Two slits for the eyes and another for the mouth.

So. They had this kinship.

He did not seem especially dismayed by this act of insolence on her part, this molting. His eyes were hard and unreal, like shards of broken glass. There was nothing like light or life in them, even though he breathed audibly behind the bandages. They were the eyes of the dead, she realized. And she had no doubt in her mind that he could murder her and feel nothing human.

He stood behind her so that, in the mirror, she was framed all around by his darkness. He put his hands out—they were thin and musical, but heavily corded, young-old, and full of rings—and set them both upon her naked shoulders. She jumped inside at his cold. The Doctor's hands swept over her, hard and learned, touching her like an artist admiring a great sculpture.

She held perfectly still as he explored every inch of her, testing the pliancy of her skin, the strength of her muscles, the limits of her modesty. She had never much cared for the touch of a man's hands on her body, the blunt, listless grappling. But this was different. This wasn't about sex. It was about possession. It was about art.

"You fixed my face," Louise said after some time. She tried not to tremble at the chill the passage of his hands left behind. "But you made me different."

"I remade you in my image," he answered simply. His voice was course, unconcerned with her observation.

She felt a jab of annoyance. "I should be dead."

"Yet you live."

For the first time, she heard his careful, burring voice and lilting inflection and linked it to an image instead of absolute darkness. She thought of splintered, moonless nights full of counts and barons moving restlessly in desiccated castles. Coaches roaring through mirror-wet London streets. Men in top hats, pinching snuff from ornate boxes.

"How?" she asked.

"Magic. Science. Which is only magic in its second skin." Slowly he spread her arms out to either side to admire her. Her body flushed, her blood shining like claret through the glasslike skin of her body. "Your face...your arms...all of it was rubbish. Hospital garbage," he said. This time his voice was tinged with interest, or, perhaps, only amusement. "Your legs I was able to repair with some little work. The breasts are your own and were and are perfect. They were not ruined."

He hesitated. "What did he do to you? What did he do with your eyes, I wonder, when he carved them from your face?"

Now she trembled. He talked as if she was a mannequin to be fused back together at a moment's whim. "Who?"

"The man who deconstructed you."

"How do you know it was a man?"

"A woman would not have carved out your uterus." He paused thoughtfully. "A man destroyed you because a man hated women."

Louise stared stunned at her Christ-like image hanging suspended there, surrounded by the Doctor's dusty, lost-era darkness. "Did you fix that too?"

"Arms and womb and face and eyes. I told you. I remade you. I made you a complete woman."

"A real little boy," she cursed.

"Stop talking like a child. I made you a woman." He released her wrists to stroke back her hair. It crackled through his ringed fingers. "I have gowns, corsets, antique combs…"

"I told you," she shouted, trembling with hate. "Fuck you. Fuck your magic."

He released her. "You try my patience, little girl." His face was impassive behind the mask of bandages, his voice as scouring as the desert. "Go away. I tire of you."

"Yes."

Without looking, he laid the back of his fingers against her cheek, softly.

And she knew in that moment that she could no more escape him and his world without walls than Adam could escape his lonely, jealous Lord amidst the tanglewoods of the serpent-infested garden.

| 5 |

Now

The moment she stepped into the studio boutique in downtown Chelsea, someone placed a dry martini in her hand and asked her to sign the guest list. With a flourish, she wrote, *Saleisha Fontana.*

The gallery was brimming with people drinking martinis and admiring the new exhibit by Bastion Lee. This was the Bastion Lee, formerly the "mad artist," photographer, and fashion designer. The only son of a British fashion model and an Italian duke with a tragic past, Bastion held the celluloid world in thrall. Saleisha had heard through a friend of a friend that Bastion had recently inherited an outrageous sum of money from a favorite aunt and had plans to retire to his summer castle in Tuscany. This exhibit would be his last.

Even though she had never met him, Saleisha knew she had to be here to see him off.

The gallery had six enlarged photographs on the walls. All were part of his Reinvention Collection. In each, a classical portrait was transported through Bastion's lens to the present day. A desolate woman in London cradled an umbrella in imitation of Monet's

Donna Parasole, a fey, naked young man (rumored to be Bastion's lover) clutched a long streamer of bedclothes over one shoulder like Botticelli's Venus, and so on. The centerpiece of it all was a photojournalist being pulled into a crowd of Taliban extremists not unlike something from one of Bosch's nightmarish circles of hell.

But Saleisha, like everyone else, was not there to see but to be seen. Amidst the patrons and art critics, she spotted Tyra Banks, Robert Pattinson, Lady Gaga, Orlando Bloom, and Elton John. Vivaldi rained down from invisible speakers set high into the ceiling.

The photo-artist-slash-fashion-designer himself, Bastion Lee stood poised in the center of the gallery, being interviewed and photographed for *Vanity Fair*, *People Magazine*, *E! News*, and the New York Foundation for the Arts.

Saleisha analyzed each of the photographs. It wasn't that she was much interested in Bastion's art, but she was determined to break the stereotype of the modern It girl. Such a girl was smart, sophisticated, and wickedly ambitious. A Janice Dickinson in Prada high heels. She was nothing like that little mouse Louise that she had roomed with back in the East Village in the time before *Clinique* found her.

A willowy girl with a rain of long, straight black hair brushed past Saleisha. She turned instinctively to see which celebrity it was.

She was disappointed.

The girl was as tall as a French model, her body slender and elongated in a mothy black affair of some foreign design, but she was far too manly to be anything but a budding actress or the daughter of royalty. Still, Saleisha instinctively checked the girl's high-necked Eurotrash rag against her own Cleopatra-inspired sheath. There was a gold asp encircling Saleisha's waist, and the neckline dived dramatically to her navel to show off to good effect the fantastic work that Angelina Jolie's plastic surgeon had done.

The horsey girl with the hair had nothing like that going for her. She was as flat as Clara Bow.

Saleisha felt pressure at her waist.

"*Cara! Amore mio!*" It was Bastion Lee himself. He was as small and slim as a young girl. His hair was jet black and slightly curling. His eyes were the most amazing shade of blue, like Caribbean waters under a storm. He wore a leather suit top to bottom, six earrings, and the faintest priestly eyeliner around his eyes. He was fantastically beautiful. "Can it be...Saleisha?" he asked familiarly, even though they were meeting for the very first time.

Saleisha put on only a brief show of resistance as he pulled her into the swarm of photographers and journalists. He stood behind her and kissed her neck like a latter-day vampire as flashbulbs went off like stars burning up in a galaxy two thousand years ago. Guests looked on jealously. Saleisha blushed but turned poetically to accommodate each greedy bite of the flashbulb.

"You absolutely must model for me!" Bastion gasped.

"But I couldn't."

"I insist!" he said, kissing her fingers. "*Ti amo*, my beautiful girl!"

Saleisha was right. This was the party of the year. Suddenly she could see an amazing future unraveling before her. Magazine layouts, her own fashion line, she and Bastion Lee walking side-by-side along the Tiber as the paparazzi followed ten steps behind, snapping off their pictures. "Oh, all right, darling," she conceded, making it sound like a weary chore.

"*Mille grazie.* Please meet me in there," he whispered smoothly, indicating a door marked Private across the gallery "And do not be nervous. You are simply invincible, darling!"

Saleisha smiled obligingly. She was certainly not nervous. She was the chosen of Bastion Lee. She was the new It girl. Soon, she would be as immortal as the art hanging on these walls.

* * *

After Saleisha Fontana, widely regarded as America's next top model, had left the gallery, Bastion Lee returned to his private dressing room where the girl in the black Victorian gown waited.

Louise stood almost lifelessly beside a glass dressing table. On the table stood an enormous vase of white lilies driving their yellow tongues toward the ceiling. And beside the vase lay a scalpel wickedly gleaming.

Away from the photographers, the interviewers, the lights, Bastion's face grew old as it often did when he shot some tragedy. He had done shots of Buddhist monks being drilled down in the Tibet Protests and had taken some of the first photographs of Hurricane Katrina and Haiti. But he did not exhibit such human suffering except among his closest friends. Only Below did they understand his art. The only real thing to be found in his gallery tonight was the death of the reporter during the War on Terrorism.

A mistake, perhaps.

He put the key to the gallery in Louise's large, thin hands. "How is the Doctor?" he asked.

"Alive," she answered simply.

"Always," he smirked.

She was one of them, one of the inner circle—and, according to rumors he had heard, the Doctor's Special One—and yet she seemed stunned by his presence. She was surprised by his humor, his familiarity, his awareness of the hidden worlds around them.

Bastion inclined his head. "The Doctor has many agents, *cara*. Not all of them live Below. Not all are society's castoffs."

She clutched the key.

His eyes softened, shone. "*Tesoro*," he said. "My broken treasure." And he kissed deeply her hands that were not her own.

* * *

The gallery was long and endlessly dark.

The moment the door clicked shut behind Saleisha, something changed. The shadows stirred. Breathed.

She turned and touched a light switch. But nothing happened; the darkness mocked her. She immediately took the doorknob in hand and turned it, but it was firmly locked. She knew she could pound against the door, but that would make a scene. Besides, there was probably a rear exit.

Saleisha turned back and looked deeply into Bastion Lee's lair. She stood upon a plain of white fur like that of an arctic wolf's. It seemed to stretch unto infinity. On the snowy plain was a scattering of black leather furnishings and high-end Nokia cameras on tripods like alien machines obtusely watching her. Over the walls were giant grainy photographs of Bastion's girls—girls on beds of forest litter, girls perched atop mountain ledges, and girls sprawled on desert sand and looking like princesses from old Egypt. And between the photographs were mannequins adorned with the new Bastion Lee collection.

She was privileged. She was seeing what nobody else saw until the very last moment.

She walked down the gallery, carefully studying every picture, every detail. Soon she came upon a small collection of light-muted images, all of the same girl in a series of unique Victorian outfits. Bastion Lee's most recent It girl, she supposed.

It was the girl in the black hair and long dress that she had seen earlier in the gallery. She couldn't believe she was one of Bastion's.

Her hips were boyish, her breasts as negligible as Louise's had been. Her clothes were a nightmare of stuffy brocade fabrics.

Saleisha paused, fully expecting to feel a twinge of guilt over Louise, but nothing happened. It was survival of the fittest, she reminded herself. Eat or be eaten.

Not very long ago, she and Louise had attended a party rather similar to this one, supposedly thrown by Kate Spade, though they never had a chance to meet their host because a pair of male scouts were circling the room, looking both derisive and somehow delicious at the same time. She and Louise always went to parties together. Two girls were better at picking out the cons and porno guys. But in the end, they both knew it was every girl for herself.

Saleisha spent all evening chatting up one of the scouts. She had to work hard, after all. Louise was a head taller than she, the big horse. She was always noticed first. But despite everything, all her hard work, an invitation for a downtown studio shoot arrived the following week addressed to Louise.

It was insane. Everything about Louise made Saleisha crazy. She was big and bony and as flat-chested as a boy. She spoke with a cloying Midwestern twang and acted like an inbreed.

Saleisha had grown up here. This was her town, her fucking birthright.

The day the letter arrived, it was Louise's late night at the trampy little stripper club where she worked the poles. She would not find the letter until the following morning. Somehow, Saleisha found herself standing over the 50-year-old toilet of their desolate little coldwater flat, ripping the letter to pieces and flushing them all smoothly away. Things should have ended there, she knew, but each time a call arrived for Louise or some dude from the club showed up on their doorstep, hopelessly in love with "Luscious Lou," a little more of Saleisha was flushed away like that invitation.

One night she snapped—a combination of cheap drink, the overdue rent, a bad break-up with her man, everything...

The point is, it all came out.

Louise should have screamed or grappled her, something normal. Instead, she just looked at Saleisha with those big, stupid cow eyes pouring over with shock and horror. Then she wordlessly locked herself away in the bathroom for two whole hours.

That worried Saleisha. She was afraid she'd find Luscious Lou floating facedown in the tub. But as it turned out, the Cornflake Girl didn't even have the guts to off herself. When she emerged, her dirty blonde hair was dyed an inky black and she was dressed in a vampy black mourning dress and dog collar. It was a big departure from the frayed blue ribbons and ruby platforms of the Dorothy costume she usually wore at the club. In the black, she looked even more trampy than usual. Saying not a word, she went off to work as if nothing had happened.

Louise was a freak.

And that was the last time Saleisha had seen her. What became of her was anyone's guess. But it was fortuitous, because, soon after, scouts started noticing her instead of horsey Louise looming over everyone else in a room. In the end, it all worked out just fine. In a way, she owed her success to stupid Louise.

Motion caught the tail of Saleisha's eye.

She turned to carefully study the wall of mannequins opposite her. She tasted the martini behind her tongue. She remembered being a kid, watching that old Kolchak episode with the mannequins, the squirm of gleeful fear. But that was fake and silly. Things like that didn't happen in the real world. They certainly didn't happen in Saleisha's world.

Yet, in spite of all this, a dummy turned its head to appraise her.

Saleisha took a half step back. She cursed under her breath. It was Bastion Lee's girl. The big one in the black gown. Was she playing a joke?

"What's going on?" she said, glaring at everything, trying to find details in the dark. "Who are you?"

The girl did not answer. Instead, she moved obliquely into the aisle, her gestures light and stepping like a Bolshevik dancer. Her face was pale like paper, her hair black. In one long, white hand, she carried a shimmering instrument Saleisha immediately recognized as a scalpel.

Finally, Saleisha experienced concern. I will turn, she told herself. I will run. I'm not some stupid bitch in a horror movie. I am not butchering fodder...

But in the end, she just stood there, watching the girl close the distance between them. Her eyes were smeary tarns in the dark—deep, but unreal. Painted doll's eyes. The girl reached out her white hand as if to grant Saleisha a sisterly touch—and then cut her sharply across the cheek with the scalpel.

Saleisha slapped her face as if killing a bug. Blood bloomed between her fingers. The world slowed. Reality readjusted itself to accommodate this unlikely madness. Saleisha finally turned to flee, but her stiletto caught in the carpeting, and her ankle turned, crippling her with spikes of pain.

She went down on the furry floor, scrambling. Meanwhile, the girl began to dance in a circle around her. The girl swirled weightlessly; the laws of physics and gravity held no sway over her. Under the long black gown, she had long, white legs that ended in small pointed shoes with coned heels, rather old-fashioned. Saleisha tried to scuffle away, but the girl twirled if she were suspended on wires, the girl encircled her, and the scalpel flicked out again.

Saleisha felt no pain, yet vines of blood flowered across the wintery plain of the carpet. Saleisha's flesh and hair licked downward into her eyes. With a groan, she reached out and ripped at the dancing, taunting legs with her bloodred fingernails, a primal desire to pass on her pain and terror.

But the legs continued to move, relentless and undeterred by Saleisha's attack, and each time they swung back into her line of sight, the wounds that she had inflicted on the seamless white legs seemed more inconsequential. The girl danced on to the music that only she could hear, unfeeling, robotic. Obviously, there was no stopping her.

It never occurred to Saleisha to cry out for help, even at the end. She was being assaulted by another woman. There was no real danger here, just a pulsating rage, a desire to destroy the source of her pain and humiliation. And she couldn't understand the trick with the wounds. Years later, she decided it was the wonder of this dark miracle that kept her down more than anything else. Like Pandora, curiosity was her undoing.

The dancer continued to twirl, slashing at Saleisha like a beautiful, maniacal music box girl. Blood and saline frothed across the carpet.

Saleisha fell back, blinded by a sheet of excruciating blood.

She was wrong about Bastion's girl, she decided. The music box girl slowly killing her was gorgeous in her own horrible, impenetrable way. As she spun round and round, strength flowed out of her like darkness cast out of a lit room. Beauty truly was in the eye of the beholder.

Then the blaze of the scalpel cut across Saleisha's vision and she saw only darkness.

***

Saleisha woke in a cold, damp room with silvery walls.

She was sore and her eyes felt sewn shut as if she had fallen asleep in her mascara. She blinked and sat up. She instinctively touched her eyes. Across the room, someone strange and yet familiar jerked in response to her.

No, not someone. *Herself.*

She recognized the mirror-Saleisha immediately. The whole wall of the tiny room was mirrored, like something in a funhouse, with dozens of mirror-Saleishas staring back at her with both curiosity and horror. She sat up creakily on the edge of a gurney and touched the bandages binding her face. There had been an accident, obviously, yet when she cast back in her memory for the exact chain of events, all she could recall was the demonic dancing ballerina—then the scalpel flicking out as brightly as the sun touching off the horizon...

She made a pained animal noise under the bandages. She pressed her fingers against her eyes. Her eyes...had been cut...

Yet, through the slits in the bandages, she saw.

She made little noises in her throat, and as if in response, a door, also mirrored, opened inward, a surreal portal of darkness. Even the ceiling and floor were mirrored, she saw. Watching the door open was like seeing reality bend.

A man stepped into the chamber. He was long and spare and dressed entirely in black. His face was similarity bandaged. Saleisha was very happy to see him. To see someone, anyone. Yet his blackened presence offered no real comfort. It was suggestive of death, Nazis, ravens. He folded his hands before him. They were large and rawboned and heavily ringed. He seemed human, yet his eyes looked no more real than the dead eyes of the music box girl.

She tried to groan out questions.

"I am the Doctor," the man informed her. "And please do not struggle, Ms. Fontana. You are still healing from your injuries." He inclined his head as if with shame. "My assistant was...overzealous. You sustained a perforating trauma to both eyes. However, I fixed those for you."

Again, she touched her eyes. She wanted to approach the man in black, the Doctor, to ask him why she was there, what had happened, why all this was happening to her, but she was suddenly afraid. He was not a man one approached without invite. She realized that instinctively. So she simply mouthed the words Thank you to him.

"It was my pleasure," he answered. Without further ado, he went out of the room, closing the mirror-door behind him.

She glanced around in wonder. Were the mirrors part of some new therapy? And the bandages...had he also fixed what that stupid cow had done to her face? The horrible unzipping of her flesh...

Her face, ah Christ...her face...

She scraped at the bandages until she found a catch somewhere, then began ripping at them manically with her long claw-like nails. There was a solid, unyielding horror in the pit of her stomach. She fully expected to see scars. She had already begun to outline the various procedures she would need to fix them. But as the bandages fell away and the chill of the room brushed her face, she realized how far beyond the merciful scalpel of a surgeon she truly was.

Saleisha screamed. She screamed long and hard, screamed until her throat tore. She screamed until all she tasted, all she knew, was her own blood, and she could scream no longer. And then she screamed some more.

All the faces in the mirrors surrounding her were naked of flesh. All of the faces in the mirrors glistened. She saw a dozen tragic ruby-red faces like a legion of Halloween masks on display. There were no doorknobs, no breaks in the walls, she saw. The Halloween Saleishas mocked her from every angle.

But unlike Jerry Pacino, whom she did not know and would never meet in this world, Saleisha Fontana did not accept her fate so easily. When it became apparent that she would not die from her injuries, nor her thirst or starvation, she grew frantic, then enraged. It took some time for her to develop the strength—how much, she could not say, weeks, perhaps years, because time meant so little here—but eventually, her relentless impacts against the funhouse walls of her prison managed to crack one of the mirrors.

She spent an eternity of cutting injuries digging through the glass to find some relief from the horror of her constant companion, her reflection. But in the end, it was an exercise in futility.

Not until she had broken away a huge shard of glass with her bare hands did she find the second layer of mirrors lurking beneath.

* * *

A second envelope, identical to the first, was deposited in the old man's mailbox the day after Saleisha Fontana went missing in New York City, never to be seen again, even by FBI agents and a legion of forensic scientists. Like the first, it carried a postal mark from New York and bore a single sheet of paper with typing upon it.

But the old man was not there to collect it. The envelope sat amidst the other cluttering flyers and mail for a very long time. The first envelope had been enough to summon him.

| 6 |

Then

The Below existed like another planet, set deep within the earth, a core unfound even by scientists and clever explorers.

There were dry concrete tunnels that rattled ominously but never collapsed. Louise assumed these ran parallel to the subway, or perhaps beneath them. There were reservoirs of water, and crates and barrels left daily in strategic common rooms carved from the New York bedrock by time, water, and perhaps human hands. There were hovels. There were people. The Homeless, mostly, the shade-like people she skirted on the street going to and from work. Once, long ago, their hallowed faces and muttering voices had frightened her as badly as any childhood monster. No more. She was now one of them.

She learned that some lived on the riverbank under the Brooklyn Bridge. Others lived deeper in the earth, untouched by either sun or sky, like the Doctor. All had their reasons. All seemed to know him—or, at least, of him. All regarded him with an unsettling mixture of awe and fear.

Louise slept in great swaths of time in the golden chamber, beneath the canopied bed. She was still healing. But sometimes she grew restless and explored the room. She found trunks of antique trinkets, old books, and a wardrobe full of dresses. She was unsurprised by the fey, antique fashions. Eventually, she came to wear them, long dresses with bustles and subdued lace, tea gowns with tiny patterns, pleats, and flounces. There were shoes, as well, in her size, but the strange, pointed walking boots were too intimidating to wear at first.

Once dressed, she sometimes walked a little way along the tunnels, leaning on two canes, but never wandering very far from the Doctor's lair. There were people all up and down the tunnels, ragged people in castoff clothes and greasy faces. Some turned to greet her; others stood silent. Some spoke softly of devils and demons. Some were, she found, impossibly insane.

Once, feeling brave, she went up and up and emerged into the shattered, bonelike remnants of an old church. The church worried her, creaking the way it did, like an old dinosaur eaten out by a fierce predator. And there was something else about it, something familiar and aching that chilled her bones. Beyond it, she could hear dogs baying in primal hunting packs. She quickly retraced her steps.

She meant to discuss the Below with the Doctor. But, somehow, that never happened.

In the evenings, she dined with the Doctor in his cavernous hall of hewn rock, the walls as golden as an egg and lit by a hundred votive candles. They spoke of history. The Doctor must have studied it extensively, for he knew a great deal. Sometimes they discussed music. He had Mary put on records while they dined. The Doctor taught her the difference between Richard Wager, Johann Strauss, and Tchaikovsky. She enjoyed the Tchaikovsky ballet music. Once he told her a story about Paganini and his haunted violin.

Slowly, as time wore on, courage seeped into her. She described her music to him, though she felt foolish talking about the Pussycat

Dolls, Nine Inch Nails, or Captain Hollywood. They did not seem very sophisticated compositions compared to his music.

"This music—you danced to it," the Doctor said one evening. With her, his voice had grown soft and somnambulistic. Sometimes he spoke in mere whispers behind the bandages and she was forced to listen carefully before answering. But the steel within remained, eyes and voice.

"I was an exotic dancer," she said, "before." She twisted the prim cloth napkin in her lap. "I danced in a club in the Bronx."

"You were a burlesque performer."

She frowned at him.

"A stripper."

"Yes."

She waited for his admonition, his disdain for such a lowly profession, but he said only, "Perhaps you will dance for me one day. To your music."

"Or to yours," she answered brightly, pleased that he chose not to judge her.

"When you are strong, Poppet," he said dismissively.

One time, long after dinner (he called it tea) she walked through a twist of tunnels and found herself in a balcony suspended over the muted, underground theater where the Doctor did his work. A homeless woman had come in earlier, thin and starved and miserable, near fainting in agony.

Louise watched through an observation window high above as he worked.

Unlike the rest of the Below, the operation theatre was outfitted with the most modern tools and furnishings available. Everything was shining and sterile, no different from any hospital.

Gowned and masked in white, the Doctor worked quickly and with a disconnected efficiency. He slid his scalpel through the wall of the woman's abdomen as Mary, similarly gowned in white, fed him tool after tool, sometimes not quickly enough for his liking. In seconds, he had peeled back the woman's flesh like a set of pale lips, and blackish blood came frothing out. Reaching deep into the wound, he retrieved a gnomish child and the ropes of the afterbirth and drew them both out, then deftly sewed up the mouth-like wound.

Louise waited to be sick, but nothing happened. Gradually, her hands migrated to her abdomen. There were no more dull echoes of pain. The Doctor's work had been just as efficient.

Back in the sumptuous bedchamber, she tried not to look at her own body, but there was a full-length mirror hanging on the inside of the armoire, and the mirror made her look, made her see. Her flesh was as firm and unmarred as that of a young child. No scars remained. She touched her slim white body and the immaculate, high breasts the Doctor seemed to admire and which gave her, at least, some small pride in her former self. She was beautiful, finally. Even the miscast eyes.

But then, she was constructed for him, by him, as the rest of this wayward world was.

***

There was an outbreak. Cholera. The Doctor was gone for several days to the shantytowns strung along the riverbanks. It was like something from an old historical novel, one where the heroine dies at the end.

He did not take Mary, saying it was too dangerous for her, at her advanced age. Of course, he did not take Louise. He did not say that it was too dangerous for her, only that she needed more time to mend, on the inside, if not out. But he must have sensed her inner panic because he gave her the key to his private library.

It was terrifyingly vast, a sheer vault full of books. There were crude shelves, though most of the books were carelessly stacked into walls and altars. They were not very dusty—she thought he must visit them often. There were candles and lanterns and, on an enormous dark oaken desk, a banker's lamp that must have been powered by a generator. Or perhaps the power was somehow cleverly siphoned off from Above. She would not put it past him.

There were medical texts and reference books and mildewing classics and bundles of yellowing paperbacks from the 1950s with bold, adventurous titles. They both looked and smelled intriguing, and she soon lost all sense of time, spending hours alone at the big antique desk, turning pages, until Mary came to fetch her for supper or to bed. She gave up her reading time only reluctantly. She had grown apart from books in the last few years, and now she was rediscovering an old friend.

Anyway, it was better than spending time with Mary. Mary was old and crooked, with bad, sunless skin and white hair pulled back severely in a way Louise had recently read about in a novel about a woman who wore her hair just so as to produce an "Essex facelift" and make her seem younger to the duke she admired. In some ways, Mary reminded her of Saleisha, her old roommate in the Village, though they had absolutely nothing in common.

She was careful with Mary. She would not make a mistake like that again.

In the evenings, after dinner/tea, she walked the tunnels, growing stronger. She used only one cane now. And she no longer fled those who greeted her. Now she greeted them back. Once, she saw the woman from the operation theatre nestled on a warm grate in the tunnels, nursing her baby. "He saved me and he saved little Matthew," she said, showing Louise the furiously suckling infant. Her eyes shone with divine worship. "He's like a god on earth."

"Who is he?" Louise asked. Matthew looked like a baby, finally, hardly like the alien thing the Doctor had pulled from the girl's body.

The girl couldn't have been much older than she. She said, "I think he might be the devil. Or he sold himself to the devil so he could perform miracles. Like in the stories of Faust."

"I don't believe that."

The girl looked sad, resigned. She did not argue. Like everyone else, she was hopelessly in love with the Doctor. Or, at least, in thrall of him. "When you find his Gallery, you'll know what he is," she said.

And so began Louise's quest to find the Gallery. She went over the whole of the library, every inch, trailing her fingers through dust and over books and cold, wet bedrock walls. She even examined the floors beneath the Oriental carpets.

But she did not find the Gallery until later after much had come to pass.

* * *

"Poppet, if you stay in bed reading all day, you will never grow strong."

She was startled by the sound of the Doctor's faint, mocking voice.

He was standing in the shadows of her bedchamber. He had come to her as he usually did, soundlessly, like the cats. She had a fantasy of him gliding ghostlike up through the floor from some lower, hellish level where he made pacts with devils. But that was absurd.

She had stayed in bed today. She was curled around a large leather-bound book she had borrowed from the Doctor's library.

He stepped to the side of her bed and took the book from her, examining it. "*The Great Gatsby*," he said. "Are you enjoying it, Poppet?"

"No," she told him. It just bothered her.

"Yet you seem enraptured."

The book was about a man who moved to the big city to become someone else. But nothing changed. Nothing worked out right. The man was a fool to think anything would be any different. She thought about saying these things to the Doctor, but he seemed to understand them instinctively.

"Not a favorite of mine," he admitted. "James Gatz attempted to change the world, instead of himself. An unfortunate man." He sat down on the edge of her bed. He had never done that before. Always he hovered properly, dourly, or sat in one of the opposing cane chairs. Strangely, he looked bruised and smashed, though no wound was apparent on him. It surprised her.

"Doctor..." she said.

"I am very tired," he answered her worries immediately. "The treatments took days."

She wondered if he had seen people die, or if he had saved them all. She thought about the girl and her infant, Matthew. She thought about what she had said about the devil. "Are the people still sick?"

"The people are well, Poppet."

She waited. She felt a quick stab of fear. Something had changed between them.

Would he throw her out? Make her leave the Below? She was healed and could walk unassisted now. He had fixed her, as he had fixed the people.

It was done, she realized. He would take away the books, the music, the safety of his inner world. She thought about the world Above, but it was now as alien a landscape as another planet. She had no place in it; it had no use for her. She had not known books or music in it. She had known only pain.

But if he told her she must leave, then she must. He was king here.

She began to cry. Like James Gatz, she was a fool.

He watched her wordlessly through the slits in the bandages. She almost felt that he was conducting some kind of inhumane experiment.

Then he spoke, and his voice was lilting, and without steel. "At the edge of dreams," he mused, "there you are. Poppet in her lion's mane of hair." He lifted his left hand and reached out to her and touched her hair, a light, moth-like touch.

She would die if she left.

She reached for him. She slid her arms around his neck and pressed her face against the stiff fabric of his coat. He smelled of the river and the Above, but beneath these odors was a cloying, meaty smell. Death, she thought, and rebirth. She drew back and put her hands to either side of his face and worked her fingers through the edges of the bandages he wore.

He stiffened at once. "Don't," he said. His voice was ancient and as cold as a blade.

The sound of it stopped her. Her heart was racing. She felt she was full of darkness and light in equal parts. "I want to see."

"No."

"Please."

He did not stop her, but neither did he aid her in his unmasking.

The Doctor was as horrible as she had expected. Each peeled inch revealed another layer of raw red trauma that hurt just to look upon. She could not imagine how he lived, or what instrument had been used to scale the skin from his face, but it had been done crudely, with a weapon blunt enough to gouge meat and knick bone. He was...and yet he was not.

She had been lucky. The man who had cut her had loved her, after a fashion. He had not stabbed into her face with such sad malice. She put the palms of her hands on the naked, glistening red meat of the Doctor's face. It immediately bled into her skin, a wound that forever wept.

It wasn't human.

He really is the devil, she thought.

Reaching, she kissed him softly.

He tasted of never-ending metallic pain. She moved closer until their clothing hissed together. She wanted to take it from him, this pain, even if only a moment of it, and hold it inside, like a flame within the glass of an oil lamp. But the rough, severe suit of darkness separated them.

Slowly she began unbuttoning his coat.

"You're a child," he said. His voice was sweet without the bandages, untainted.

"No, I'm not." Louise kissed him again. She kissed his mouth until his mouth changed, softened, accepted hers. She touched his hair, thick and rough and uncut at the collar. It had been golden once, the hair of a prince in a fairytale. Now it was dusty grey like old daylight, the color of blond kept too long in the dark. She buried her face in his throat, his unmarked flesh there scented by libraries and comforting old attics full of half-remembered treasures, old times, simpler times, that belonged in tintypes and cameos.

He made a groaning noise in the back of his throat.

She drew back and lifted off her nightdress like an ill-fitting skin, then lay back on the pillows, watching him watch her.

"Don't seduce me," he said. His voice was cracked and weary with age.

"I love you," she said.

"I fascinate you."

She held his unflinching gaze. "I want to be with you forever, Doctor."

A bitter smile pulled the bleeding meat of his lips apart. "My Daisy. My Juliette. My Guinevere?"

"Yes," she hissed, showing her teeth.

He leaned forward, his hands to either side of her, and kissed her throat. She thought it must pain him, each shuddering touch of skin on non-skin, yet he showed no discomfort. Perhaps, given time, she too would be like this, all cold iron and tempered steel, unbreakable, painless. She gasped as his kiss inched slowly downward over her reconstructed body.

Desire saturated her. Blood beaded and streaked her whiteness of flesh from the angry red wound of his face. She did not mind it. His lips painted her breasts, her belly, the soft, childish down between her legs. And when he finally touched her at her core, she shuddered violently, as if in pain.

"Please," she said. "Please, Doctor. I love you."

He was against her, as hard and deadly as the night or some weapon. His absence of a face loomed inches above her. She turned her head away so as not to see.

"Look at me," he said. His voice was sharp, like a slap.

She looked. His blood wept onto her face like teardrops.

"Will you think of princes, Poppet?" he asked, his voice suddenly angry. "Knights? Lancelot?"

"I don't want princes," she told him, moving with him. Her voice sounded raw as if she'd been screaming for hours. "I want you."

He pushed her roughly into the soft flesh of the bedclothes and took her there. The root of his passion cut like a blade within her. She did not mind the pain. He kissed her harshly, sucking her tongue deep into his mouth as he moved her, moved inside her, her pain building ever upward like the ruins of the old church that she had visited Above, ancient and pale and reaching high toward a god that had forsaken them all.

***

She lay inside his embrace for a long time afterward, his face in her hair, his arms clinging to her ribs. She wanted him. She wanted to touch him constantly. She was sore with want, with yearning. But, for now, he slept like death.

So she made do with examining his pocket watch. It was beyond an antique, scalloped and engraved with strange symbols and Latin and Greek words of wisdom. Inside there was a myriad of arms and configurations. The underside of the clamshell held a scratchy, yellowing picture of a young woman in dark, high-necked attire. She was almost supernaturally beautiful, flawless, like a white lily in ringlets of black hair. Louise thought of spindly actresses from gossamer silent films.

She felt a splinter of annoyance. Was this the Doctor's dead wife, or a long-lost betrothed, cruelly taken by fate, like in his books?

"She was Lizabeth. My partner," he said in the shivering cup of her ear. "And my maker. An amazing scientist. Mata Hari with eyes of coal."

Louise stiffened at the devout sound of his voice.

"She wasn't mine," he explained. "We were perfect friends, siblings in science. But Lizabeth was not taken with men. You understand."

The tension inched away. Louise felt very foolish, jealous of the dead. "She's gorgeous. The most beautiful woman I've ever seen. You should have made me like her."

"I told you, Poppet. I remade you in my image."

She turned deftly on the bed so that she was lying beneath and he atop, his arm pinning her arms to the pillow above her head. His face did not disturb her now—if, indeed, it ever had.

"How?" she said. "How can you live?"

"The same as you, Poppet. The Elixir preserves us both."

"The Fountain of Life," she said. She touched his impervious white flesh under the open shirt and solitaire. He had a good body, not frail or weak like the bodies of so many academics. It was the body of a man just blossoming into mid-life, hard and wise. But he was much older, she knew.

She had read about the Elixir in his hand-written journals in the desk of the library, but, at the time, she had thought he was writing literature. In the journals he and his partner, the beautiful, enigmatic "L"—Lizabeth, presumably—ran a private practice for the lower class in the London borough of Whitechapel. The city was described nothing like the Jack the Ripper movies Louise had seen. There was no fog, no romance, just rain, endless waste, despair, and deathless poverty.

Having both grown up under similar conditions, the Doctor and Lizabeth were determined to discover a formula to defeat tissue rejection and overcome blood type, which had only just begun to be studied. Given time, they might be able to eradicate syphilis and other popular social diseases. Limbs and organs could be repaired, or even replaced, under the right circumstances. Blood would not need to be typed at all—it could be swapped indiscriminately between persons. That was their dream.

To that end, they had developed the Elixir, a formula they had stumbled upon by mixing a number of mundane chemicals in specific quantities, though the Doctor's notes did not specify the ingredients. It preserved any living creature exactly as it was in its present state, seizing its cells up *ad perpetuam* and disallowing the progression of disease, aging, or tissue rejection. They felt it was a good find, potentially beneficial to mankind. They began their experiments on insects at first, then rats. Then, as success followed success, they moved their way up the evolutionary ladder until they were ready for the ultimate test.

But only a few days before the Doctor and Lizabeth were prepared to treat an ailing prostitute with the Elixir, something happened. The narrative became erratic, then writing ceased altogether in the journal.

She touched the Doctor's face with just the tips of her fingers. He did not flinch. "What happened to Lizabeth? And to you?"

He considered her request. She was afraid he did not trust her enough to reveal the rest of the story. But, finally, he spoke, and his voice was breathy, with none of its former steel.

Shortly before the experiment with the prostitute, he said, their dream came to an end. A police captain by the name of Pymm was alerted to their activity by one of the "sack-em-up" men they employed to steal corpses from fresh graves so that they might study human anatomy in more detail. Professional grave robbers were untrustworthy by nature, and most had criminal records and were not fond of police. But in this case, a grave robber had fallen in love with Lizabeth, and when she did not return his affections, he turned the two of them in to the police.

The lab was raided by Pymm's men, and the Doctor and Lizabeth were arrested. Grave robbing was a serious charge in those days, and they found themselves facing the gallows. And it all might have ended there and then, and ended grimly enough, but Captain Pymm, like so many other men, fell under the charms of Lizabeth's beauty. Once alone with her, he forced himself on her.

Lizabeth had long proclaimed herself the equal of any man. And she was in matters of science and academics. But her grandmother had been from the Far East, a former Geisha, and Lizabeth was delicate, frail. She had suffered consumption in her youth. She was unable to fight off Pymm's advances.

But Pymm, whose mind loved beautiful women but whose body did not respond to them at all, became enraged when his rutting with Lizbeth didn't culminate in anything. He blamed Lizabeth, of course. He was like a feral dog, said the Doctor. He beat at Lizabeth's face again and again, smashing it like a ripe fruit. Finally, the Doctor, who was being held in an adjoining cell, managed to wrest Pymm back against the bars. This being Whitechapel, the Doctor kept a scalpel hidden inside the lining of his coat sleeve for protection. With it, he cut Pymm's face and struck out one of his eyes.

Pymm, a direly ugly man to begin with, went into a bloodthirsty frenzy. With several of his men holding the Doctor down, he used that same scalpel to carve the skin from the Doctor's face one slow inch at a time—crudely, the blade growing duller with each strike. Finally, he drove the blade deep into the Doctor's liver. The Doctor began bleeding out black. Pymm and his men, frantic with horror at what they had done, fled the scene. In the confusion, Lizabeth was able to lead the Doctor outside to a coach.

Later, in Lizabeth's underground laboratory beneath the London streets, the Doctor himself became the subject of their first human experiment. Lizabeth fixed his terrible internal injuries as best she could, but there was nothing she could do about his face. He needed a blood transfusion immediately, and she and the Doctor were not the same type. Had she waited to infuse him with the Elixir, he would have died from loss of blood.

So it was done. And the Doctor was made *ad perpetuam* on that day. And on every day that followed.

***

"And me?" Louise said when he had finished his story. She wondered what part she played in his drama.

"And you," he answered, his disarray of stiff fabrics rubbing deliciously against her nakedness as he bent over her, to kiss her sweetly and bitterly, "are like me now."

| 7 |

Now

Hade's Gate teetered at the very edge of the Bronx, near the waterfront, a sunken brownstone with a skin of arcane graffiti, a garish red door, and a raw-knuckled doorman named Odin. Odin distrusted men but liked women. He had been married for thirty happy years and had three daughters.

He thought he knew the girl who looked like a black-haired lioness from somewhere, but he couldn't recall where exactly. She was big, legs that went for miles, and she moved like an athlete. She wore a witchy micro-dress with bell sleeves and polished scarab-black boots. Her black hair cloaked her to the base of the spine. Had she had a broom or a pumpkin she would have been perfect. As he took her money and stamped her hand, he glanced at her pale leonine face and long cattish lashes. She was beautiful, yet strangely guileless and primal, which only added to her charms.

Only after she had been swallowed up in the room of liquor, smoke, and catcalls did he remember Louise, sweet Louise, whom he called Cheese Louise, and who always smiled like a little girl at his joke. She had gone on to better things, he hoped, things well beyond this rattrap. He hadn't seen her since that night so many weeks ago, the night she danced as if she was exorcising spirits, then left with that geek Tim.

Better she was gone, he thought. Yet a part of him ached for her, as he might his eldest daughter.

* * *

Nicholas Lazlo, the illegal Romanian-immigrant-owner of Hade's Gate, noticed the girl in black almost at once. She was leaning against the bar, her endless legs crossed girlishly, a whiskey sour on the bar in front of her. She stirred the cherries around with a straw. The first thought that hit Lazlo was, Louise is back. Luscious Lou! His barkeep, Tim, always put two extra cherries in Louise's whiskey sours.

Lazlo missed Lou. Girls came and went in this joint all the time, but Lou was one of a kind, a born dancer the likes of which Lazlo had never seen except in some of the secluded Roma shantytowns outside Bucharest, the girls with handmade tambourines and broom skirts who danced as if they were calling spirits. Louise had danced just as wildly on the stage. She had given Lazlo a steady stream of patrons, obsessed fans, and stalkers.

In three strides, he was there. But when Lazlo reached the bar, he immediately realized his mistake. This was a different girl whose lank, leggy frame only reminded him of Lou. He felt a dull stab of disappointment, followed by a longer, more invasive incision in his brain and groin that he could only conclude was primal, red lust. Unlike Lou and her almost childish innocence, this girl was sex—sex walking in a pair of platform boots.

"Hello, beautiful girl," Lazlo said, leaning against the bar. He gave her a fatherly, concerned smile. "What is your name?"

She turned to look at him.

The girl was striking rather than pretty. Her eyes were endless, like something one could fall into and drown—and oddly mismatched, which only made him want her more. When he was thirteen, Lazlo had lived with a second cousin with just such eyes. Over a number of dull, sweating summers, they had fucked frequently in a shed just outside the house.

The girl blinked slowly, like a lizard. "Lizabeth." Her voice was a course, simmering voce sotto.

"Liz, then. This your first time, babe?" Lazlo was very proud of his fabricated Brooklyn accent.

Liz looked toward the stage where several of Lazlo's girls were shimmying around a small copse of steel stripper poles. "I'm looking for work."

"You dance?"

"Yes," Liz said. Her eyes locked on his as she plucked a cherry from her drink and sucked it slowly past her fingers like a piece of candy.

Lazlo felt most of his internal organs turn over. The human part of his mind whispered a faint warning, that this girl was simply too good to be true, but the animal part was already taking over. His leather jeans felt very tight.

"Do you think I could do that someday?" Liz asked, referring to a girl who was on her knees on the catwalk, shaking her ass to a techno-remix of a popular Rob Zombie tune and skinning snakelike out of her costume.

"I think beautiful girl can do whatever she wants," Lazlo answered with a breathless smile. "Why not see what the other girls are doing? And later we see if you have 'what it takes?'"

"Yes," answered the girl in a sibilant whisper. Again, she blinked in that slow, hypnotic way.

Later, after Lazlo had closed the club, Liz whipped seamlessly up and down the stripper poles. She even supplemented her silvery modern dance moves with a shocking assortment of on-point and arabesque gestures that made her seem to float on the bridge of Billy Idol music snarling out of the speakers above.

Lazlo thought of the fleet-footed strigoi of his homeland. Spirits clothed in human flesh, luring men into their pale, deathless embraces. "Eyes Without a Face" would forever remind him of Lizabeth, he decided.

This girl. She was *Swan Lake* and rock and roll all tied up in one delicious, jewel-lipped, long-legged package. Definitely a keeper.

And the extended lap dance she gave Lazlo afterward wasn't too bad either.

* * *

Near morning, Louise returned to the creaking ruins of the church and went Below, chased by premonitions of dawn. She found the Doctor wandering the library, paging liberally through his dustless tomes. Had he waited up for her all night?

No, that was ridiculous. He must be researching a new disease to treat, she thought. He could not be so obsessed with her. Not as she was with him.

She went down into the gilded, fairytale bedchamber and stripped away the witch dress. She slept naked now, with the Doctor, in their bed. She lay down on the bed and buried her face in the pillows that smelled of him.

She slept. But with time, she became aware of the Doctor's presence, insinuating, like nostalgia. It pressed against her, made of all sharp-edged fabric. She liked his clothes, liked to feel them against her raw skin in a way that was far more intimate than any mere nakedness could be.

She turned herself into the Doctor's body, looked into his face. His cold metallic mouth came unto hers, intimate and familiar, a comfort.

"Once more above," she told him as he moved his bloodstained kiss over her face and down her throat, "and it will be done. Lazlo hired me."

He fell still in her arms. He felt cold, removed. He changed, just like that.

"I have to," she told him. "I have to do it. You must understand, Doctor."

He had remade her body, her mind. Even her way of speaking was changing, like something from Charlotte Bronte.

But the Doctor did not immediately respond. She could feel his reluctance and his rage. It was a familiar, palatable force between them. His hands coursed absently over her body, and his clothing hissed against her. Yet he was apart. "Did you dance well for...Lazlo?" he finally said.

"You're jealous."

He tried to move evasively aside. But in one liquid dance motion, she had him. She climbed atop him, holding him down against the mattress, trapping him from running from her. He was hard against her. She smiled. She leaned down, her hair tenting them in together, and kissed him hungrily. The blood of his face roughed her lips. She dipped her tongue into his mouth. She tasted blood there too; he had been biting and chewing his tongue.

"I didn't sleep with Lazlo," she told him as she moved, first with him and then against him. "I touched him, Doctor, but I didn't sleep with him." She wasn't that type of girl.

His eyes flared with rage. He reached up and snagged both her thin wrists in one of his hands, holding them apart for the moment. "Where?" he demanded. He sounded hoarse, scornful, and his face and body were full of writhing vengeance. The hand that held her was electric. "Where did he touch you, Poppet?"

She told him. And he touched her there as well, like an anointing.

And everywhere else.

* * *

Lazlo was as happy to hand out props to his girls as a pervert is to hand out candy to playground children.

At her request, he had two stripper poles set up on the central stage, and between these, he extended a heavy chain, and from that chain, he hung a child's swing with a plain metal seat. He let her pick her own music. She chose Queen. It was danceable but had a touch of neo-classicalism to it. The Doctor would be proud.

Dressed in her neat, short parochial dress and knee socks and pigtails, she swung back and forth over the heads of the patrons, the glass heels of her stripper platforms chocking in rhythm against the stage to "Another One Bites the Dust."

The patrons watched like a collection of silent, slack-faced mannequins as she wriggled butterfly-like out of her cocoon of fabrics, revealing more—and yet, somehow, less—of herself to them. She leaped from the swing and hit the stage on her platforms, dressed in little more than frayed threads. But she wasn't seeing a collection of flushed, desperate, drunken men-faces swaying with her hips and with the contralto baying of Freddie Mercury.

She was far away, underground. She was Below. And she was seeing him. She was gowned in black and silver brocade, and he was dressed in his brushed black evening suit from 1933 with its satin lapels and standing collar. They met in the middle of a high chamber full of lighted chandeliers, rust-gold walls, and mournful Chopin. They were waltzing in wide, even circles, hands entwined, rings clinking together.

The club patrons were on their feet, this hungry tide of sweating, desperate male flesh. Were it not for Odin up front, several of the more desperate young men would have crawled up onto the stage to touch the hem of the new girl as if she were a female messiah descended to earth to save their forlorn souls.

But Louise did not notice their admiration. She did not notice any of this. Swaying to the music echoing inside her own head, lost in an abyss of time and shadows, she waltzed off into the backstage.

**

The girl on the swing.

Tim couldn't stop thinking about her, even as he scrubbed down the bar and cleared away the myriad of sticky-edged glasses and overfilled ashtrays.

Earlier, when the stage lights had first come up, he hadn't noticed her, not at first. She was tall and model skinny. She looked like a Catholic school whore. Tim assumed she was like all the rest. Her face was homely, strong, unforgettable amidst a rain of glittering black hair hanging down in pigtailed ropes. Another farm girl who had escaped to the big city, head full of childish dreams, here only to fail. Now she was shaking her tits for a bunch of geek boys who could only get it on with the monthly centerfold or some computer-generated bitch.

Then the music sprang up and everything changed. Tim saw. And Tim thought she might be the One.

A thirty-two-year-old native of New York City, Tim had seen it all. He was nothing like the hungry dogs who visited the Gate nightly, sniffing up the skirts of the girls. He was the very antithesis of just such a man. He was the big brother of the joint. Everyone talked to the barkeep. He was good at what he did.

Lazlo's girls liked him. He walked them to their cars at night. He drove them home if they were too drunk or stoned to be out on their own. He saw their littered, trashy little apartments, met their impetuous lovers. He knew it was important he surrounded them with compassion. He even told them he was gay—they opened up more easily that way.

But her. The One. For her, he might open himself.

She was different. Like Louise, she had a sweetness inside of her, just one hard-packed by vinyl, gloss, and makeup. He could see it. He had the sight to do so.

But thoughts of Louise made him cautious. He had thought she was the One, once. And he'd been wrong.

Louise. Lou.

Tim had known almost everything about her, almost from day one. He knew about the false driver's license she used to dance at the club, and that she used cover-up makeup to hide the fact that she was a cutter. He knew she collected stuffed monkeys and her favorite color was yellow. He knew that she liked three cherries in her whiskey sours.

Yet how much had he really known about Lou? Sometimes he wondered.

He often tied a yellow ribbon around the stem of the glass when he served her. He didn't even know why he did it; it just seemed like the thing to do, something old-fashioned and childish. It delighted her, brought out the little girl under her dirty New York exterior. In his fantasies, she collected the ribbons, keeping them in a drawer by her bed, waiting for the day to show him.

But he had been wrong about Louise. She was neither sweet nor naïve. He learned that painful truth one night a few weeks ago.

She'd been crying when she first came in to do her shift. He slid a drink down the bar to her, but it did no good. She was nearly hysterical, ranting about her roommate, about some talent scout letter that was lost.

"I can't stay here anymore, Tim. I've got to get out of this place," she sobbed, clutching her head as if it might topple off her shoulders.

"I've always said that," he told her as he polished a glass. It was the truth. "You're too good for this place, Lou. Too good for Lazlo, that skank. Do you want me to drive you home?"

She shook her head of inky black hair. She had dyed it recently. He was disappointed by that. It made her look pale and hard and doll-like. He had always loved Lou's flaming blonde hair under the harsh strobe lights. "I have to go on. I need the money."

And so she had. But in the middle of a complicated twist onstage, she stumbled over the chair she was using as a prop. It was a bad sprain, and she was limping badly when she reached backstage. Tim immediately steered her into the backroom to collect her coat.

He started driving her back to her apartment in the Village, then made a sudden decision and turned off onto Jerome Avenue, toward the projects. He hadn't brought a girl home in ages. He had promised his mother that he wouldn't. But everything was out of sync tonight. Why not this?

Lou was reluctant, but not worried, not then, and not until the end. They knew each other too well. He was the girl's big brother.

"I have ice for that ankle. Let me take care of you," he said after he had pulled the car into the lot behind his apartment building. He leaned against the headrest. He was tall and slim in his black, soft barkeep's garb. His hair was carefully cropped once a month, close to his ears, which were a little too large and the source of much derision when he was a child. His mother used to tape them. But he had bedroom eyes. Everyone said so. Large, black-lashed, almost girlish, like a soap actor. He tilted his head at her. He reached out and abruptly beeped her nose.

Lou was suddenly laughing and crying at the same time.

"It's not the end of the world," he told her. "Whatever it is."

He led her up to his place. It was small, but meticulously kept through the Big Cleaning, done monthly, like his haircut, and the Small Cleaning, or "picking-up" (as his mother called it), done once daily. There was delicate white china in cupboards, fashion magazine fans on the end tables, and a music and TV center that could be closed away to look like an English wardrobe. Lou investigated the cuckoo clock and the pictures on the walls, men in old-fashioned dress and cavalry uniforms, and women in flapper gowns. He did not tell her they were all purchased in yard sales and antique shops.

He made her a strong drink in the galley kitchen and retrieved ice for her ankle. He made her sit on the sofa, scrunchy with plastic —the only thing he didn't agree with his mother on. Girls disliked the plastic, even though Mother was right about it keeping the sofa stain-free. "Hey," he said to Lou, urging her to sit. By then he was anxious with desire.

Things went downhill fast. She didn't want him fussing over her, she said. She didn't want a neck massage, and she seemed appalled by the idea that someone—he—would want to kiss her. He even confessed that he wasn't gay, to no avail. Insult gave way to anger. She acted annoyed, then betrayed, as if he had lured her up here under false pretenses. As if she didn't dress like a slut and dance on Lazlo's stage every night, advertising herself. As if she didn't like it, flashing her tits and cunt at those dogs in the audience.

Louise got up to leave.

Tim grabbed her arm. He only meant to plead with her to stay, but somehow they wound up wrestling down on the sofa like two kids sparring. She kicked him somewhere in the groin. He was dizzied by pain, not himself. He struck her a glancing blow across the face. She fell back against the armrest, dazed. He wrapped his hands around her throat. It was soft and gave under the smallest pressure.

She began to choke. But after a while, she stopped and went all blank and lifeless under him.

Tim was certain he had killed Lou. He scooted back on the sofa. "Mama," he said, and then louder, as panic unwound within him, "Mama!"

But his mother wasn't feeling well, he knew. He thought she must be asleep in the bedroom.

He had just started wondering about what he was going to do with Lou's body when her eyes suddenly flared open. She was alive, but too weak to move. She could only make rasping, hiccupping noises through her bruised throat.

He couldn't let her go. She would tell.

He carried her into his bedroom, to the bed. She was hardly down a second when she sprang up like a cat and started fighting him in earnest. She could not cry out, but her long nails raked over his face like claws. He held her down. She grew wild, possessed. But now he was angry. Everyone thought he was skinny, weak, but he was much stronger than he looked. Especially now. Her arm broke like plastic under his firm grip. She made mewling noises, and again she passed out.

He pushed her down, wrestling with all the silly clothes women wear, and pushed himself inside her. He had never had real sex with a woman before. He expected to feel something supernatural, like in books and movies. He expected to feel the universe spinning out of control. Instead, it was all sweaty work and no fun at all. He didn't even come. He grabbed Lou by the scalp and shook her violently like a giant rag doll, but she was out cold.

He left her to clean up in the bathroom. It took maybe five minutes.

When he returned, Lou was gone, lurching like someone gut-shot into the hallway of his apartment building. He lunged after her, but she had made it to his neighbor's apartment and was pounding frenetically at the thin piece of plank board that passed for a door in this building.

"What is it? What do you want?" His neighbor, Jerry, called hoarsely through the skin-thin door. He and his wife Nora went to bed early, Tim recalled. They'd be angry, and they might remember details later on.

Lou made gargling sounds out of her crushed throat.

Disguising his voice through his hand, Tim said, "She's seizing." It was the first thing he thought of. "It's the drugs."

He waited to see what would happen, if the old man would call the police or open the door. But Jerry, like Tim, was a native of New York. He knew better than to poke his nose in other people's affairs. And as he suspected, the door never opened.

Tim dragged Lou back into his apartment. She was almost spent by then. She collapsed inside, panting and bleeding from somewhere down there all over his clean white carpet.

"You cunt," Tim said when he saw the staining. "Look at the mess you've made." His mother would make him do the Big Cleaning now.

He dragged her by the hair back to his bedroom. She bit his hand as he hauled her up to the level of the mattress. He slapped her down to the floor. The pain in his hand had made him mean.

He kept expecting the sex to get better, but it was just Lou mewling and writhing beneath him. All she did was bloody his clean white sheets. He stopped and put some music on in the living room, tuning the stereo to a heavy metal channel and turning the volume up to cover any sounds Lou was making.

His bedroom looked like a warzone when he returned. Somehow, Lou had found the strength to drag herself to the closet. The closet door hung open and Mother lay dustily on the floor on her face, the clean dress Tim had dressed her in that morning tangled around her waist, which was unacceptable. One of her fragile old arms was cracked at the elbow, and when Tim lifted her carefully into his arms, he saw that her mouth hung open and voiceless as it always did, but now she seemed to be screaming in pain. His anger boiled.

"You hurt my mother," he told Lou.

Lou shrank against a corner of his bedroom. She looked like one giant bloodied bruise, and he wondered how he ever thought her beautiful. She was a mess. He stalked toward her. She lifted her good arm to defend herself. He saw, more as an afterthought than anything else, that she had a baseball bat she had taken from his closet.

He caught it mid-swing. She had almost no strength left, and the act pitched her forward, into his legs. Tim bunted her back against the wall, the thudding music covering the soft, deep sound of her body's impact in the soft plaster. He raised the bat, bringing it down like a sword over Lou's shoulder, over her good arm. Her body vibrated from the impact, but she hardly reacted at all. It was as if she was made of wood. Her eyes saw him blindly, like bloodied white jewels in her pale, icy face.

After Tim had smashed both her arms to pulp, he thought about breaking her legs. He had seen that once in a movie. But Lou had really beautiful legs. It was the first thing you noticed about her. He just couldn't bring himself to do it. Like Lou, his mother had done ballet, once upon a time.

Lou was finished, anyway.

After he had put Mother back into the closet where she couldn't see him with the girl, and had turned off the stereo, he tried one more time with Lou, but he was soft. It wasn't going to work. Obviously, she wasn't the One his mother had told him about, the One who would one day make a man of him.

He went to the kitchen for the bottle of wine he kept at the back of the refrigerator. He'd kept it there for years, for the blessed day he'd found the One. But he knew now that that would never be. Mother was wrong. He uncorked the bottle and poured the wine down the kitchen sink. Then he returned to the bedroom with the empty bottle.

By the time he finished with her, Lou had been violated many times and in many different ways with the bottle, first whole, then broken and full of teethy shards.

* * *

The girl on the swing was waiting downstairs by the curb when Tim stepped out of Lazlo's club.

Earlier it had started raining in miserable grey sheets, a typical New York industrial rain. She stood as close to the eaves of the club as she dared, but in a way that allowed her to spot the late bus on the street.

She gripped a newspaper over her head. She had an amazing figure in her wet, tight-belted raincoat. And streaming all over her was a thick, wet spillage of black hair that seemed too delicate to belong to a human being. It looked more like fairy hair. Doll's hair. Her face was white, her eyes black with makeup, and her lips as pink as seashells. She was simply gorgeous.

Tim scuffled across the puddles on the sidewalk until he reached her. "Liz, right?" he shyly asked.

"Yes," she answered. But she did not look at him. She was glancing into the street.

"What bus are you waiting for?"

"The 41. To the Bronx."

"You missed it. Sorry."

"Oh." It was a soft, lost sound. Obviously, she was new to the city. She didn't know the beat the way he did.

"I can give you a lift. My car's around back. I mean," he said, pouting in a way that brought out his bedroom eyes, "if you're okay with that."

She continued to stare into the street, as if willing the bus to arrive. She seemed very childish. Almost virgin. Maybe she was the One? Could Mother have been right after all?

She turned to him. "All right."

* * *

He led her into his darkened apartment. It was very neat and orderly from the Big Cleaning, and all the stains had been scrubbed out. The sofa with the scrunchy plastic had done its job. Not so the bed; that had been replaced.

He closed the door, and, reaching past Liz, touched the light switch.

There was a harsh click, but nothing happened.

Outside there came a belly growl of thunder. The power was out.

Liz turned to face him. She looked at him strangely with bright, fever-dark eyes. She blinked only once, slowly. She had really amazing eyes, even though they weren't the same color.

Tim felt a dizzying wave of desire. In the dark, he kneaded his crotch with one hand. With the other, he started to reach for her. But Liz's slow gaze moved obliquely to the left.

Tim looked.

A strange man stood in the shadows of his apartment. He was tall, spare, unmoving, but darker than the darkness all around them. Even though this was New York, Tim did not at first think of burglars. He thought of Louise. Had a friend, a relative, or perhaps a hired investigator, found him out? And what would Mother do if he went away to prison? Who would take care of her?

"Who are you?" Tim asked in a choked whisper.

Lightning snapped at the room like a rabid dog. For one second Tim saw the man clearly. Tim had never seen silver eyes before, nor such a carnivorous hatred.

"The Doctor," answered the man.

Tim immediately voided himself into his clean, pressed trousers. He opened his mouth to scream, but Liz seized him, covering Tim's mouth with one delicate hand. This is silly, he thought. Her strength was debilitating.

"You cunt," said the Doctor behind the shroud of bandages masking his face. His voice came from deep within his body, like the best British actors, but the voice wasn't human. It was too elemental. It was like the thunder outside. It was like a wild animal that had learned to speak. His metallic eyes inched downward, considering Tim's soiled crotch. "Look at the mess you've made."

Louise, he thought. Louise had come back. And she had brought a doctor...

As a child, doctors had always frightened Tim, gowned in bleak white, armed with prickling instruments. His mother used to bark at him furiously to sit still.

Tim's body surged with fear. He bit down hard on Liz/Louise's hand, but she did not remove it, nor did she cry out in pain. It was like biting soft plastic.

The Doctor grabbed Tim by the hair, jerking his head to one side, pushing his body effortlessly up the wall. Tim's scalp screamed in agony. Jesus Christ, he whimpered, then chastised himself. His mother did not like him taking the Lord's name in vain.

The Doctor pressed close. Tim squirmed. To his upmost horror, the Doctor was hard and aroused against him. Tim heard the appalling sound of the Doctor's tongue slowly churning in his mouth.

"Doctor..." Liz/Louise warned, standing close beside them.

"Yes, Poppet."

"He's mine. You promised."

Another epileptic shock of lightning lit the room. Tim saw that the Doctor was grinning behind the bandages. It was a sight more demonic and unnatural than he could endure.

"As you wish, Poppet."

They were the last words Tim heard before he passed out.

| 8 |

Then

Beneath the sounds of a Mozart sonata, she heard him enter the library.

Sitting cross-legged on the floor, Louise looked up from her book about a Russian princess fleeing from revolutionaries, then over at the record player in the corner. It wasn't quite a phonograph, but it was still very old, a tarnished antique like everything else. She willed it to stop because everything in the world was required to stop when he entered a room. But the tinkling, surreal music went on and on.

The Doctor was carrying an ornate brass candelabrum with him. She thought they only existed in movies about haunted castles and opera houses. He set it down on the mantel beside the record player, then reached for the needle, stopping the music abruptly.

"Am I disturbing you, Poppet?" he asked.

She let the book slide out of her lap. She could not read or listen to music when he occupied a room. She could do nothing but wait patiently for him to speak again.

"Mary is preparing a special tea," he said. "And I have something to show you."

Louise stood up, smoothly, and without effort. Tonight she wore a long bustled dress of deep emerald velvet that looked plush in the dark, like soft cat's fur. There were a hundred buttons up the back. At first, when she woke that morning, she had felt intimidated by the sight of the dress lying across the foot of her bed.

Ever since that first night with the Doctor, she had found a new dress waiting for her in the morning, Doctor-chosen. She didn't mind. She had called for Mary, and the old crooked witch came impassively into the chamber, her face as blanked of emotion as a medieval portrait, and buttoned the dress up for her without even the slightest nuance of interest. Tonight, before bed, the Doctor would unbutton it, his lips and fingers brushing each newly exposed inch of her skin.

She followed him into the bedroom where he had, inexplicitly, laid out a new dress for the evening. This one was made of creamy white beaded satin that shimmered like water. Unlike the others he had chosen for her, all masterful haute couture reproductions manufactured in France and Japan, this one was truly an antique. She knew. She felt a wave of fantastic nostalgia.

"It once belonged to Lizabeth," the Doctor explained. "It is the only thing of her I have left."

Louise waited patiently beside him.

"Will you wear it tonight, Poppet?"

He had never asked before, only commanded.

"I couldn't," she stated simply. "I might tear it."

"Do you mean to tear it?"

"No," she said, appalled by the very idea. "Of course not."

"Then wear it."

He came to her, undoing the buttons on the back of the green velvet dress, efficiently. The touch of his fingers sent pulses sounding deep within her body. But he did not help her don the white dress; he only watched.

It fit well, though somewhat snugly in the bust, and the hem fell at least three inches too short. In his time, she would have been showing her ankles, which would have been unacceptable. The Doctor had said Lizabeth was small and delicate. Louise was neither.

He stood over her, admiring the dress, running the smooth of his fingernails along her cheek, an absent touch she instinctively turned into.

"Mary will see to that. The dress can be let out, the hem taken down. Then the dress will be yours."

She hesitated. "Was it Mary's, the dress?"

"I told you. It was Lizabeth's dress."

"But did Mary wear it?" she asked. "When she was younger, I mean?"

His fingers grew still against her cheek, coldly burning. There was a malicious glee in his eyes. "Are you always so jealous, Poppet? Do you dream of all the hundreds of little girls I have plucked from the river, only to seduce and throw away when I tire of them?"

He was mocking her. "How many?" she mocked him back. She loved him, but she would not be cowed like Mary, like the rest of the subjects in his underground kingdom.

"I," he answered, "have lived over a hundred and fifty years. Do you think I am so virginal? A priestly vampire trapped in amber?"

"Stop it," she said through ground teeth. "Stop hurting me!"

He continued to touch her softly, yet his voice was as cutting as his blades. "I can do whatever I wish with you. You are so easy, Poppet. Wind you up, set you loose. As easy and malicious as a hungry Whitechapel whore…"

Her hand lashed out, clasping the Doctor's throat like a necklace of primitive bone. She pushed forward, through the seething cloud of her rage. Then she was against him, and he against her. She did not stop. She kept surging forward. Her strength was enormous. But there was little room to move.

Together they hit the wall of the library. The wall shuddered. He did not.

He only stared down into her upturned, sweating, bestial face as if she were doing absolutely nothing to him. His complacency, as much as his invulnerability, enraged her.

She screamed. She screamed until her throat tore and blood coughed over her lips. She screamed for herself and she screamed for every woman who had ever been butchered to unlovely shards in a dark corner of this city. It wasn't a human sound; it was akin to an animal baying. Her elbow jerked upward, thrusting the Doctor up the stony wall. He felt light as air to her; she used almost no effort at all. She held him, her arm vibrating with power. She could have held him a million years and never tired.

Then she saw what she had done, the horror of it, and she let him go.

He felt lightly to his feet, unperturbed, the cat that he was.

Not so she. She crumpled to her knees. She was no cat. Just a girl of heavy bones, blood, and bruises. She covered her face with both hands and began to rock back and forth, there on the carpet with its swirling arabesque patterns, keening through her fingers, the sound coming nonstop like vomit.

It all went on for some time.

* * *

She awoke on the floor of the library where she had fallen in a heap of aging brocade.

It was late; the tall, flesh-colored candles of the candelabra had burned down to amputated stumps. The shadows were deeper. There were no days or nights underground, of course, but there were shades of darkness. Shades of grey. She heard the bass growl of the grandfather clock standing lone sentinel beside the bookshelves.

So. It was midnight, the witching hour.

He was sitting in the wing chair where she often curled up to read his books during the day. He was watching her, waiting for something.

She touched the bodice of Lizabeth's dress. Her hand found a frayed edge. "I tore it. I tore Lizabeth's dress," she said from the floor. She started to cry all over again.

He waited. And when he had observed her long enough, when she had cried enough, he said, "You're awake. At last."

She hiccupped. "I want to die."

"You won't," he answered. For the first time, his voice sounded tired, even human.

"There must be ways. Methods. I can't be this. I can't be sixteen forever."

He watched her with calm indifference. In the near-perfect dark his eyes shone like wet sea stones drawn up from a tremendous depth. "In one hundred and fifty years I have found no ways, Poppet. No methods."

She could not move. She weighed a thousand pounds and she was a hundred thousand years old. She would never move again. "You should have let me die," she said at last.

He thought about that as if it made good sense.

"All your books," she went on, "all those girls...Anna Karenina, Juliette...they found a way out. They weren't this...thing."

His eyes blinked, seemingly alive, or it was only a trick of the light. "There is no choice for you now but to continue as I have continued."

"I can't," she said. Her voice was husky and cracked like old glass, like Mary's voice. "I'm not strong like you." She waited to sob, but nothing came. She was too empty.

He stood up smoothly. The shadows became a little brighter when he moved away from them. "Then I will make you strong, Poppet," he said. "Come."

His voice pulled her up like wires.

***

Within the grandfather clock, there lurked a door. It would have been invisible to even the most trained human eye. The seams were invisible, and there was nothing to give it away except for an innocuous keyhole that resembled one of the numbers. The key the Doctor kept with him at all times, on a long gold chain around his neck.

He unlocked the door and, carrying the candelabra, pushed inward.

She hesitated. Beyond the secret door lurked an almost prehistoric darkness. The dank underground walls were cavernous, the shadows big and jagged. There was a smell of ancient grey tombs, an evil, almost reptilian smell. Instinct told her to flee.

Yet she remained fastened in place until her eyes adjusted to the deeper darkness and she picked out the rough, grave contours of a tunnel hewn right through the very bedrock of the city.

"I call it the Gallery," said the Doctor. He stepped aside for her.

She took a hesitant step. Then another.

She stopped. She could go no farther.

The Doctor, sensing the hopelessness of luring her on, took her hand. He stepped boldly through the doorway. Within, immersed in her terror, she felt a curious excitement. Perhaps he had sickened of her. Perhaps she was to be incarcerated like some forlorn, troublesome princess in a story.

A kind of electricity came from the Doctor. She felt the tingling of it in his hand. Like her, it was a commingling of terror and excitement. She let him lead her on. It was probably not for the best, but she was part of his electricity, caught up in the web. There was no escape.

The walls were colorless and bleeding with water. Little musical notes chased them down the narrow corridor full of frightening, iron-banded doors. It was almost perfectly dark, even with the candelabra. Her foot came down on something squirming that quickly scampered away. She let out a hiss of surprise—she never had been much of a screamer—and stumbled.

The Doctor steadied her. "Take heed."

"It's dark," she said stupidly. She was irritated. If he was finished with her, why didn't he simply thrust her into a cell and be done with it?

The Doctor took her arm as if they were going to dance a minuet and walked her through a plush carpet of rats that skittered past the hem of her dress. They made almost no sound, only a dull hissing noise as their claws raked the floor in escape. She was not afraid of rats. The cats in the Doctor's lair kept them in check. And, anyway, a greater danger lurked at her side.

They stopped at a door. He took her hand and placed it upon a primitive latch. So here now, she thought, the journey ends. It was almost a relief.

"Open it," said the Doctor. He was very close, his body flanking her on one side. She heard the soft roar of his voice in her ear and through her skull and all down her back.

Her fingers played over the latch. She might be faster than he; it was conceivable. She might be able to turn and outrun him, lock him within the tunnels, he and his little key.

"Poppet," he said, "open the door."

"Why?"

"Because I want to show you horror."

His voice rushed through her to the floor this time. Had he reached inside of her, through the petticoats trimmed in clever lace, through knickers and flesh, he could not have drawn out her lust any better. She took the latch in hand and opened the door at his command.

Inside, darkness glittered, parting for her now dark-sensitive eyes. She saw a short man dressed in rags wandering the cell aimlessly, bumping into walls. At first, she wasn't alarmed, only curious. Then she saw that he wasn't very short, not really. It was only an illusion. He was not short, but headless.

She had never seen a headless body before, certainly not one that walked—maybe in a special effects movie somewhere. It did not seem real. It moved mechanically, lurching from one wall to the next like a robot. Stop. About face. Repeat. It grew maddening after only a few seconds and she found herself turning away.

He misinterpreted. "You are disturbed?"

"He's horrible," she said flatly as if she was speaking of some pesky little brother who was bothering her.

"You don't sound convinced, Poppet."

"How?" she asked. "How have you done this?"

"How else, Poppet? The Elixir."

She found the glint of his eyes. She held them, a changeless shine. He did not blink. Then again, neither did she, unless she wanted to. Perhaps they no longer needed to blink or eat or sleep or breathe, and did so only from reflexive force of habit. If he was not going to thrust her in there with that thing, if he was not going to imprison her, she would need to explore these concepts further.

"Was he...is he...?"

"That is the body of Captain Pymm," said the Doctor.

The shock was bleak, sudden, a dull knife thrust. Yet it didn't surprise her.

He reached out, past her, and pulled the door closed. The lock engaged. But if she listened carefully, she could still hear those slow, dragging footsteps sounding endlessly through the old stone walls.

"Let me show you the rest."

There were other cells like the one that housed Captain Pymm's restless body. Some were people—or might have been, once. Most were pieces, farms of eyes, hands, hearts, other organs, quivering chunks of jelly flesh that skittered along deep watery tanks like strange deep-sea creatures. They were not aware, she thought, or hoped. They just were. Curiously, there was no frightening equipment, no horror movie set pieces. There was just the Elixir, in tubes, tanks, and syringes, preserving all.

She touched each door, peered into each cell, explored every tank. She studied every creature or half-creature, the shocking hopelessness of every small horror spiking through her body in echoes. Yet it awakened a strange, listless curiosity within her, as well, and she wondered if she might one day assist the Doctor in his experiments. It would be interesting.

She was not afraid. Parts of her had come from these body farms, he said. Without them, she would not be whole.

They reached the last cell.

"My brave Poppet," he said. He reached out and touched her hair. She put out her hand, to touch him touching her, but he suddenly took it and drew it down until her fingers rested on the latch of the door.

With a swallow, she bravely opened that last door.

Immediately, some great creature lunged at her.

The Doctor slipped between her and the beast, soundlessly, with that great catlike agility of his, and the beast stumbled back in fear. As with the first creature, at first, she found she was mistaken in her observations of it. She thought it was a wild dog of some kind, vast as a lion, its dark fur savage, and the muscular, wolf-like body certainly suggested that. But nestled in the mane of the neck was a human head with one egg-white eye peering out at her, a human head that writhed, full of human hate.

She felt sick.

"Pymm," she said immediately. She put both hands to her lips. It was he. The Doctor had said he was a dog. The irony fit. It was correct.

Turning, she fled.

* * *

Somehow, the Doctor was past her, blocking her escape from the library. He was quick like all of the things were who lived by night. She pulled away and came around, but the Doctor had her as if all this had been choreographed in the past.

He cupped the back of her head. He wanted to kiss her, but the bandages were between them. He turned his head instead and buried the coarseness of the fabric against the pulse in her neck. She felt like she was falling within. She gave up. Gave into it. She thrust herself against him, her flesh instinctively seeking its maker. She did not care. Yet, she was screaming. Screaming and crying hysterically, like some god-awful heroine in one of his books.

He clutched her and she hung limply in his embrace, the doll that she was. He drew both hands down her body, touching her intimately through Lizabeth's golden-white dress. Then he drew back, to gauge her reaction. To study her, she his science.

She felt angry, sick with loss.

He looked on her cruelly, flawless in his monstrosity.

"Let me die," she said.

"No," he answered. "Never."

She struck him across the face, rending the bandages along his cheek on one side with her hooked nails. Scarlet glinted out, the surreal landscape of his ruin. He grunted but did not cry out. He only raised his long surgeon's fingers to the patch of wetness there, then brought those fingers around to his mouth, to lick, as he watched her through the little slits in the bandages.

"Fuck you," she said, stumbling back away from him. Her voice was scorched from her screaming, barely more than a breath. There was no strength left in it. Then she corrected herself, she *articulated*. "Fuck you to hell. I hate you!" she screamed. "I hate what you've done to me!"

"What a nasty, cruel little bitch you are," he said. He did not sound altogether displeased. He reached for her. He took her by the arm and threw her back against the bookshelves so forcefully that a line of books winged to the floor like dead angels. She didn't feel a thing. He came unto her again, but it was all he could do to hold her still, such was her strength.

But he had her. And he, too, had strength.

He held her placidly against the books with one hand, and, with the other, reached through her writhing skirts and lace and found her core. She grunted at his ungentle touch. "My beautiful, my lovely one," he told her. "Fight me if you can."

His words only made the desire worse. Inside this cage of nightmare, caught up in his web, she wanted this fabulous monster. She wanted the Doctor.

He knew. He always knew. He pushed himself, the source of his power, deep inside her body. She screamed even though there was no pain at all; she was too ready for him.

She grappled with him until the fabric of his clothing rent under her nails and she felt his unnatural cold seeping forth. She thought of that perfect, horrible, impervious body, the face of the monster, and inside it all, the hard, pure tyranny of princely desire.

"You're hurting me," she said, moving with him.

"Yes."

"Hurt me. I want you to. I want..."

"What do you want, Poppet? Articulate..."

They came together, suddenly. In that last moment, she saw Pymm, felt the sweet, saturating vengeance of the Doctor's handiwork. She hated him, his perfect circle, his completed story.

"Revenge," she screamed.

* * *

And two days later, after all her plans had been set, all her designs perfected, Louise dressed for the academy where Jerry Pacino worked as a janitor.

And so it all began.

| 9 |

Now

Tim came to in the dark. He at first thought he was at home, in bed, and everything else was a dream, but the hardness of the bed beneath him made him think of morgue slabs in movies where private detectives investigated strange crimes. He sat up slowly and found he was, in fact, lying on a gurney of some ancient, rusted design. Had the police found him passed out in his apartment and rushed him to the hospital, the victim of a mysterious assault? And if so, where was Mother?

The gurney creaked ominously as he moved. The walls dripped. He did not think he was in a hospital.

The room he found himself in looked like someone's forlorn basement. He got to his feet, nearly sliding on the wet cement. His mind swirled, making him grip the sides of the gurney for support. Maybe they had found Mother and had sent him away to some grim asylum like when he was a kid. They didn't understand how Mother lived beyond death.

When he was ready, when he could walk without pitching forward, he tried the only door in the room. It was unlocked, which he thought was odd. They did not often leave doors unlocked in asylums. He knew that.

He pushed against it.

A chill breathed over him and through his clothes. The room let out into a crumbling flagstone hallway of some medieval design. Perhaps, he thought, he really was dreaming. His last coherent thought was of a man all in nightmare black touching him...he shuddered.

A part of him urged him to run, but he sensed things in the dark, squirming.

He found the lighter in his pocket. He did not smoke—it was an unacceptable habit to Mother—but many of the girls at the club did. He thumbed the butane wheel until he caught a flame.

The hallway, he discovered, was a writhing carpet of rats. He gaped involuntarily, wondering where in hell he was, what he could do. But the rats quickly scrabbled away from the light, leaving the floor as bare as if no rats had been there at all. He knew he had to get out of here, whatever this place was.

Cupping the flame to protect it, he started mincing down the hallway, his direction random. Sounds pressed in, driving him on ever faster and more desperately—strange, muffled whimpers, sounds neither human nor animal.

He hit a door unexpectedly with his shoulder, and he cried out. Somewhere in the darkness behind him, something growled as if in response, a sound so human—and yet *in*human—he felt his bowels clench and nearly give out. Reaching, his hand fell on a rusted metal latch. The muffled noises persisted, strange high murmurings that sounded like human speech. Something was in here with him, something larger than a rat, larger than he was, something trying to speak to him. He scrabbled crazily with the unfamiliar mechanics of the latch until it, like the first door, swung open.

Tim lurched forward, into blinding light. He landed hard on the floor, his teeth clacking against the rough stone tiles. He grunted in escalating horror. Something was crashing down the hallway behind him, banging bones and muscles against the narrow walls, its cries razoring over his skin. He flipped himself over and saw a great black beast with chips of glinting eyes in a human face charging toward him.

He would not have believed it could exist were he not seeing it now, with his own eyes. He rolled himself over so he was on his back and out of the way of the door and instinctively kicked out, slamming the door closed on the nightmare barreling down on him like a runaway locomotive. A latch snapped home and a moment later the door took an enormous hit, as if with a sledgehammer. But it seemed to hold against the assault. Tim paddled against the floor like some overturned turtle until he found his feet, then slowly rose in a half-crouch.

That's when he saw he wasn't alone.

They were here, waiting for him.

He saw the girl first, Liz—who was also, somehow, Louise. She wore a long, funny-looking dress of shiny brocade and ugly, old-fashioned shoes. He was not used to seeing so much clothing on Louise's lank body. With her was the man from the apartment, the one who had held him effortlessly against a wall, and he was even more fantastic and horrifying. In this vast room full of old books and flickering gaslight, he looked like a warlock secreted away in a tower somewhere, weaving mischief and spells.

He was seated in a straight-backed chair with Louise sitting across his lap.

Tim burned. The familiar way the man touched Lou, running his heavy, beringed hand up her leg and then up the bodice of the gown, made it clear to Tim that they were lovers, that she was his. The touch said *mine*. The touch said *suffer without*. The man in black, the one Lou called the Doctor, looked directly at Tim as he touched Louise, savoring Tim's agony. His face was terrible—not the bandages, but the dreadful, shining glee in his eyes.

"So you," said the Doctor, his voice hypnotically deep and scorched, the sound of a piece of machinery cranking over, "are the one who violated my wife."

Tim took a step back as if physically pushed by the force of the voice alone. His back hit the horrible door with the horrible thing lurking behind it. Yet he was immovable as if the voice alone held him there.

He looked at the Doctor. He looked at Lou. He didn't recognize her at all. Yet, somehow, he did.

Louise stood up, her gestures fluid, unreal, and moved to the center of the vast chamber of books. Her face was different, but he would have recognized her moves anywhere. She stood like a ballerina in the first position. Meanwhile, the Doctor, who seemed to think himself her husband, moved to a table where an old record player was waiting.

He dropped the needle onto a vinyl record. After a moment, music pounded out.

Tim expected something old, surreal, something his mother would have approved of, but the music was surprisingly modern, a rattling dance beat similar to what he heard played at the club every single night.

As he watched, dumbstruck by the strangeness of it all, Louise started to dance. She slithered slowly out of the long gown and began to prance around the wing chair in the center of the chamber, dancing the way she always had at the Gate, with all the life and energy she had—even though, by all rights, she ought to be dead and at the bottom of the East River. How had she survived? Tim himself had taped the bloody remnants of her seemingly lifeless body into a large disposal bag before dumping it into the frothing black water.

Yet there she was, Louise—and yet, not-Louise—thrusting her gyrating ass into his face, then whipping around in a pirouette and stalking toward him in her funny, old-fashioned shoes as if they were big, clunky stripper platforms, drawing so close to him that he could see her unblinking, mismatched eyes. Smiling sweetly, Louise snapped her teeth at him. Tim jerked back, banging the back of his head against the door behind him.

The record played on. Louise slunk down to her hands and knees and crept forward like a prowling lioness, then flipped onto her back and rolled her spine across the floor, undulating her ass and thrusting her legs out into a deep *V*. She brought her heels down on the floor resoundingly, arched her back and flipped over onto her feet in a limber little move that very few girls could pull off, even after a lifetime of dancing.

Tim opened his mouth to say something, to ask how it was even possible she was alive and walking, but Louise spun around him, surrounded him, then suddenly thrust him backward into the wing chair. Her strength was irresistible. Then she was right there, right in his lap, facing him and writhing to the music, her powerful dancer's legs clenched up tight around his waist.

Tim realized he was about to get the first lap dance of his life—and all by a living-dead girl. He wasn't sure if he ought to be thrilled or appalled by the idea.

Louise's hands, her lips and tongue, were all over him, leaving ghostly snail trails of cold wherever they touched. One of her hands cupped the back of his skull. The other slid snakelike past the belt of his trousers. Tim lunged within. He had never come before—at least, not with another person. It was almost a relief.

Louise smiled. Her teeth looked as hard and gleaming as chips of bone.

Then Tim felt a deep, unfelt pain rip across his groin and stomach. He looked down at his crotch and saw that Lou held something in her hand that resembled a piece of mangled, bloody hamburger. There was a gaping black hole that began somewhere just south of his belt buckle, a hole bubbling forth a bloody froth. In her other hand, he saw, she held a glinting surgical scalpel. This she deftly inserted into his new, homemade cunt. There was a soft sound as she slowly unzipped the musculature of his waxy white abdomen in a long wet line. The tubes of his intestines slithered forth through the slit in his belly like frightened snakes escaping a cavern.

He felt too stunned to react. And, anyway, there was no pain.

Louise seized him at the throat. Her face was stone, even her smile. She stood up, pulling him up her long, tall body as the music played on carelessly. Tim's body pulsed with the beats and with blood loss. Louise was taller than he, taller than most men, though not taller than the Doctor; Tim's head rested on her chest. She put the scalpel, cold and hard and bloodstained, against his throat.

Tim held very still. He was already dead. He could not survive such horrible wounds, he knew—and, anyway, he didn't want to. Louise had made him come, made him a man. She was the One. It was done. He did not struggle.

The record began to skip. Louise let him go.

Tim fell straight to the floor, watching the blood pour from the great mouth-like cavity of his body. He was concerned, but not for himself.

He was unhappy with Louise.

She had been so innocent, so naïve. Once. What had the Doctor done to her?

With his failing strength, he put out a hand to grasp the toe of one of her weird, old lady shoes. But Louise stamped her foot down hard on Tim's wrist, holding him apart even now, holding him immobile.

The room became kaleidoscopic with lights. Beside Louise stood the Doctor, the man who had remade her. He wielded a syringe, which he gave to her. The sight of the needle dragged a primitive terror up from Tim's body that echoed out of his mouth in a long, jagged scream, like a delayed reaction to his disemboweling.

Lying pinned and helpless, he scratched at Louise's shoe, but she was like iron. She was immovable. "Louise," he begged. "Louise...please...please, Louise," he said like a song, "let me die..."

"I assure you, Tim," Louise said as she bent low, the syringe biting deep and insect-like into his spine, "your death is the last thing on my mind."

* * *

After Louise had replaced her dress and fixed it properly, she carried Tim back to his cell.

Pymm did not approach them as she walked down the long stone throat of the hallway, though he did make queer snuffling noises in the dark. He was much too afraid of the Doctor.

She placed Tim on his gurney, then stood against one leaking grey wall, near the door, her arms hanging lax at her sides, and waited. The Doctor said the Elixir could take up to twelve hours to circulate through human blood, bone, marrow, and down into the precious, hidden DNA molecules, where it did its finest work.

Time passed, but time did not reign here.

Slowly Tim came around, which was rather bad for him. Rats had been gathering around the foot of the gurney for some time—there were no cats permitted in the Gallery. Tim groaned under the heavy drugging effect of the Elixir. Louise remembered well the dreamy, leaden feeling of it.

In time, he lifted his head. It fell back with a crash on the gurney as if decapitated. He let out a rattling curse, then tried once more.

This time he made it. This time he sat upright.

His flesh was ragged and gaped like an envelope. He shuddered and touched the empty, deflated cavern of his bowels. He suddenly passed out. But when he came around again he was a much wiser man. He did not touch himself this time. He turned his head, instead, and eyed Louise.

His eyes were as vast and wild and unseeing as Pymm's. "You bitch...you fucking cunt!" he wheezed. "What did you do to me?" For one clear moment, rage overcame all over instincts, even those for self-preservation, and Tim pitched himself forward in a vague attempt to reach her.

Louise stepped backward.

Tim landed crumpled on the floor. A wave of rats parted for him, then came together again, like water.

Louise waited patiently while the rats did their work. It took much of the night.

Near morning, Tim, or what had once been Tim, creaked on the floor at her feet. Every piece of flesh, every string of soft viscera, every organ had been raped from his body. He was little more than a wet red skeleton. His skullish head clicked back and forth as she approached him, and the naked jaw dropped open in fear, but no sound was possible.

She lifted him up in her arms—he was as light as a toy—and placed him back on the gurney. A rat clambered up the side of the gurney and raced through the hollow cage of Tim's ribs. Without really noticing, Louise turned and exited that place of the damned, shutting the door soundly behind her.

* * *

"Where is the Doctor?" Louise asked when she found Mary in her room, hanging her newly laundered clothing in the wardrobe. She knew better than to speak to the old woman except out of necessity. But now that her work was through, Louise needed to find him immediately.

She needed to know if he meant what he said about her being his wife. She needed to know if they could move ahead together.

Mary turned, her mouth pinched, Lizabeth's dress—now Louise's—draped across her arm like a forlorn pet. "Don't you know? You're always with him."

Louise stood immobile, the scalpel in her sleeve already sliding down into her hand. If she had to kill this woman to make her understand her place here, then so be it. If the Doctor was king, then she was queen. Not a consort, but an equal. She took a step toward Mary.

Mary, sensing the fission in the air, looked away. "He's Above. In the church. There's been an intruder."

Concern sickened Louise. The Doctor never went Above except under cover of night. If he had done so this morning, then there was substantial danger, something unavoidable.

Gathering her skirts, Louise raced away down the warren of tunnels like a heroine in one of the Doctor's beloved books, escaping from the castle keep and up, up to the place of destinies.

***

The bones of the Church of St. Bridget lay in disembodied ruins.

There was nowhere that was safe. It was all a death trap. Only one window remained, a tall portal that depicted a white dove against the blue glass, carrying an olive branch. It was weathered, cracked. Sunlight pierced the window in thin swords that reached down to shards of shattered wood that had once been a pulpit.

Dust swarmed through the hot daylight and pricked Louise's eyes like hot tears as she climbed a barely serviceable staircase and burst fully through the door and into the ravaged body of the church. It had been a long time since she had seen daylit sky and flooding light. She felt like running, some unholy beast, until she found shelter underground, but the Doctor might need her.

She spotted him immediately. He stood under the window of the dove, his footing familiar and confident upon the fallen girders. He was an unwelcomed black blot against the dull golden walls of this sanctuary. One arm was uplifted in what might have been mistaken as a salute to the rising sun. From it dangled an old man by his throat, his toes inches above the rubble.

"You dare," the Doctor was growling, "come here?"

Louise slowed her pace. She was quickly losing interest in the present drama. If some transient had trespassed, stirred the Doctor's ire, that was not her concern. The world Above was now the complete antithesis of her concern.

But then the old man lifted his dirty head, and Louise saw and hesitated. The man was not very old, she realized. Unwashed and unshaven, with lines of sorrow cutting knifelike through his face, he only seemed so. He saw her. He looked at her, dismissed her, and then looked back at the Doctor. He did not recognize her, of course, as Tim had not. Not at first.

"My daughter's here," the old man croaked. His voice was broken from alcohol and disuse, his body weak from neglect. But indignation had made him brave in the end. "I know she's here. I want to see her. I want to see my daughter...!"

"And how, sir," answered the Doctor, drawing the young/old man close to his blankly wrapped face and seething eyes, "can you be so certain of that?" He had a scalpel already in hand. He held it like an extension of his own body, though the stranger could not see it. Neither could Louise, but she knew it was there, nonetheless.

"Stop," said Louise, suddenly.

She saw the Doctor relax his grip on the man, but only a fraction.

The man stirred. "She sent me a letter!" he screeched. "I have a letter from her!" He ripped at his clothing awkwardly until an envelope was torn free, creased and stained from alcohol and urine.

Louise felt sick. She lifted her skirts and picked carefully over the broken debris until she was standing at the Doctor's side. She picked up the plain white envelope.

Inside there was indeed a letter, as the man had said. She read it through. In it, she, Louise, begged the man to come find her here, at the Church of St. Bridget, claiming she was the prisoner of a madman. The Doctor immediately dropped the man, who curled up on a bed of rusted debris and fallen rebar and began murmuring to himself like any other drunkard in this city. The Doctor turned to approach her, to take the letter.

"Did you do this?" he asked.

"No."

He took her ungently by the shoulder, his great power pressing into her body on all sides. His eyes ripped into her like blades, searching to extract the truth.

She held her ground. She was his Poppet, perhaps, but not his minion. Not his Pymm monster. She was not afraid of him. She glared back. "Mary must have sent it."

"Mary," he began, "would not..."

"Mary had my things, my addresses. She was the only one who knew about...him." It was all she could say of the man clawing at the debris to retrieve his beloved letter. "She loves you, Doctor. They all do. Of course she sent the letter." She turned the full force of her burning eyes, Doctor-made, on him, so that he would see she spoke the truth. "I told you," she said softly, "I want to be with you forever."

His strength lessened around her. He believed her, at last. "Louise," he said, the sound of her name hissing past the bandages. "He is your father?"

The old man had found his way to her. He pawed at her shoe, the way Tim had earlier. "Louise..." he murmured through his drunken haze and swollen mouth. "Where is Louise...?"

"No," she answered the Doctor. "I don't have a father." She crouched down before the old raggedy man, the last remaining link between herself and her old world. She took his chin in her hand and directed his eyes upward.

He looked. His eyes were a faded harvest brown, as hers had been, once upon a time. The eyes were what she remembered, though the body had changed, withered. Once he had been a big man, able to force her into a closet or to hold her down against a bed and undo her at will. No more. Now she had power.

"Old man," she said through her teeth, "Louise is dead."

His eyes gradually registered the impact of her words, but he had nothing to say to her. She was not his Louise.

The Doctor came up behind her, very close. The scent of time enwrapped her. "We could take him below," he suggested. "What fun we could have."

Louise stood up smoothly and reached for the Doctor, clasping his arms about her waist. His strength entered her through that simple touching. "He's already in hell," she said. "There's no more we can do."

Turning, she led the Doctor Below. Later, she knew, after they had enjoyed tea and had retired to the golden bedchamber, they would together devise an appropriate punishment for Mary.

BRIDE OF DOCTOR FAUST

| 10 |

Below

Louise bent over the young man in her bed and bit into his cheek like it was a new golden fruit. The boy's eyes fluttered, but he was otherwise oblivious, his living meat rendered painless by generous amounts of local anesthetic. She watched the wound seep for some moments before lowering her face and kissing the rose-red wound. Then she bit the wound itself.

"Poppet, please," said the Doctor. He had already administered more morphine to the boy than was healthy. She knew from assisting the Doctor in a number of procedures that any more might stop his heart. Then he would require the Elixir to survive. And then he would be as they were.

Impervious.

Timeless.

She stopped biting and simply writhed against the bloodstained bedclothes, a familiar heaviness growing in her loins. She held her arms out to him and the Doctor came unto her. He kissed her, licking all the young man's blood from her lips. Louise sat up, embracing him there on their bed. Deftly she liberated the scalpel from his suit pocket and slid the tip beneath the mask of bandage he wore, the keen edge splitting the cloth with no trouble at all. He grunted at the pressure as the bandages came off in red pieces, the little flesh remaining on his face sticking to them in reptilian patches.

"Does it hurt very much, Doctor?" she whispered, pressing herself against him, against the hard, changeless body of the man who was her husband. Her godly creator. Her hand moved smoothly down the front of his body and she found him through the thick black armor of clothing he wore. Her touch enlivened his body, though his face remained impassive as always. There was little flesh or musculature there to make it otherwise.

"It always hurts, Poppet."

She wound her arms about his neck and her legs about his waist. "Then I shall have to kiss it to make it better." And she did. Forgetting the boy bleeding on the bed beside her, she ran her lips and tongue and sometimes teeth along every newly revealed inch of the Doctor's non-skin, the slick, red-wet bones of his face, the raw patches that tasted of new-minted pennies. The Doctor groaned under her ministrations, his hands tightening about her. She bit his cheek and he hissed fiercely through his teeth, his sudden hardness pressing into her. Their mouths clung in a kiss and she drank the blood off his naked, bleeding lips. Soon enough, he was holding her down and thrusting into her harshly, as cutting as his infamous scalpel. She grunted from the violent impacts, her Timeless body unperturbed by the force. She took him and he was cold, so cold inside her.

A soft knock on the door of their bedchamber interrupted their reverie. Louise loosened her hold on him, and the Doctor edged backward off the bed. He turned his back and reached for a hat on the wall beside his wife's vanity, there for emergencies such as these.

Louise sat up, arranging her sodden nightgown around her legs properly. "Yes," she answered politely.

The door opened and Rachel peeked in. She was young and slender, no older than Louise, but there was age in her eyes and in the etchings around her mouth. There was a disconnected wisdom in her words. Once a girl of the streets like she, the Doctor had helped deliver her son, Matthew. He had saved both their lives. Ever since, Rachel had become as loyal to Louise as a lady-in-waiting to a grand duchess. "Sorry," Rachel said, glancing down. "There's someone here to see the Doctor."

Louise glanced aside at the Doctor standing with his back to them both. "A patient?" She moved to the foot of the bed while gathering her blood-soaked skirts about her like a nest of loose skin. She often acted as nurse and assistant to the Doctor when he saw new patients, but she was sure no one was scheduled for tonight.

Rachel looked distressed. "I don't believe so. I mean..." She searched for the proper words, practically wringing her hands in the process. "What I mean is...she doesn't look like she's in need of medical care."

Louise stood up, subconsciously insinuating herself between the Doctor and the door. "She?"

"A woman, ma'am."

"If she doesn't need care, then what does she want with the Doctor?"

"She's requesting an audience. She said the Doctor will see her." Rachel glanced aside once more at the Doctor, standing prim in his unbreathing silence. "And she says her name is Lizabeth."

Dr. Lizabeth Montgomery was standing soldier straight near the wing chair in the Doctor's library when Louise stepped into the room. The sepia lights made her look as colorless as an old photograph, and the flames of the hearth backlit her, so she seemed equally dark and full of light.

So this is she, Louise thought. *The Great Architect of Us All.*

Lizabeth was as slender as a child, and not very tall, but she had a presence. She wore a suit of black clothes, was fitted with a waistcoat and ruffled neckcloth, black leather gloves, and a black hat. From beneath the brim of the hat streamed black crinoline that fell in an almost impenetrable curtain to her chin. Louise wondered if she had traveled like this through the streets, terminals, and airports of the modern city Above, or if she had affected the uniform of her time only after arriving Below. Perhaps, like some immortal vampire, she had hypnotized all those she had encountered and they had seen nothing out of the ordinary.

Long ago, in a time of hansoms, opera boxes, and vignettes, Lizabeth had aided the Doctor in inventing the Elixir which had saved and perpetuated them all—she, the Doctor. Louise, obviously. She and the Doctor had toiled in the worst slums and poorhouses of the East End for years, working in secrecy to create an end to the suffering of Syphilis and other diseases of the time, but things did not work out the way they should have. They never did.

A police officer by the name of Pymm had collared them, imprisoned them. They were scoundrels in the eyes of their contemporaries, gravediggers and corpse-stealers. They were to be hanged on a charge of immoral behavior when Pymm, an overzealous brute, had forced himself upon Lizabeth. The Doctor had retaliated with the scalpels he kept secretly sewn in his coat sleeves, slicing Pymm's face, blinding him. Pymm, enraged, had commanded his men to restrain the Doctor, and with those same impossibly sharp scalpels had degloved the Doctor's entire face an inch at a time before embedding one long, silvery blade in his liver. In the chaos that ensued, Lizabeth was able to secret the Doctor away, but she had been forced to use the Elixir to preserve his dying body. She could not fix his face. There was no time.

He was made immortal on that night. And on every night that followed.

That was the story the Doctor had told her. Louise hadn't known that Lizabeth lived. Or, indeed, that Lizabeth was one of them. Timeless, as she had come to think of herself and the Doctor.

Lizabeth was one of the Timeless.

Louise forced herself to breathe slowly in and out. She had been married to the Doctor in Lizabeth's gown. The Doctor spoke of her often and with great affection. No, she wasn't prepared for Lizabeth.

Lizabeth had been beautiful, unearthly. Or so the Doctor had told her. In some ways, Lizabeth was indeed like a beautiful vampire. Lizabeth had made the Doctor what he is, and the Doctor had made her. They had passed the torch of lighted darkness down from one to another.

Lizabeth stood tall and erect in her all-black, eyeing Louise critically from behind the veil. "Where is he?" she asked. Her voice was harsh, unmusical, but not unlikeable. It carried snippets of the East End of London, along with other places, and, presumably, other times.

"The Doctor will see you shortly," Louise answered stoically. They were the words she used on all new patients, though of course, Lizabeth was much more than that. The Doctor needed a moment to replace the bandages; Lizabeth would not rush him.

Lizabeth's eyes narrowed behind the veil. "Does he tell you to say that?"

Louise held perfectly still. She was wearing a dark pine green dress in sparkling brocade, one of the finest she owned, her long hair showering her all over her shoulders like black rain. And yet, somehow, she managed to feel ugly—and small, despite towering over Lizabeth by inches. The woman in the veil marched forward on her tall, inky boot heels and Louise felt an instinctual need to shrink, like a child expecting a blow to fall, yet she forced herself rigid. She closed her right hand into a fist, feeling the straps there that bound the knife to her forearm.

Lizabeth stopped with inches separating them. Her analytical gaze pressed relentlessly against Louise. "You are she, child? The Doctor's Poppet?"

Louise forced her voice up. "I'm not a child."

"You look like a child. You are dressed as a child. The Doctor is perverse."

"I'm not a child. I'm his wife," she insisted.

Lizabeth's hand flashed out, much faster than Louise had expected, and snatched at Louise's loose hair. "If that's so, you ought to wear your hair up as is befitting his *wife*."

Louise stayed rigid. She told herself that Lizabeth could do her no harm. Even if she broke every bone in Louise's body, they would not stay that way. Lizabeth could cut her up into a hundred small pieces and those pieces would live on, invigorated by the Elixir. The idea was both revolting and interesting at the same time.

Lizabeth smiled, or rather her posture did. Louise did not know what her face was doing, if she even had one. Long ago Pymm had broken it in his rage. Perhaps the Doctor had restored it. Perhaps Lizabeth herself had fixed it. Or not.

Lizabeth took a step forward so their bodices touched. Louise sensed the unnatural chill beneath the suit of clothes, the feel of things both dead and deathless. Lizabeth was smaller than Louise, more fragile-seeming, like a woman made of black glass. And still, Louise was afraid. Lizabeth's gloved fingers touched Louise's reconstructed face, her lips, her throat, then parts further down. "Very pretty, my dear," she said approvingly, and Louise slid the blade in her sleeve loose a centimeter more.

"Lizabeth," came the Doctor's hard, echo-less voice from behind them.

Lizabeth eyes simmered and her hand dropped. "You do excellent artistry, William," she smirked. "As always."

***

"I love her eyes. So innocent. But her mouth reminds me of a Whitechapel slut. What was your inspiration? Federico de Madrazo y Kuntz?" Lizabeth asked, accepting a tumbler of brandy from the Doctor. Louise had expected she would take tea, like heroines in Charlotte Bronte novels, but she had requested a drink, instead. Lizabeth took a seat by the hearth, owning her space the way a man might, and swirled the glass.

"Albert Lynch, actually," the Doctor responded. He took his place beside Louise on the velvet chaise and, reaching forth, laid the back of two fingers softly to Louise's cheek. "She was a blank slate when I found her. Little more than mimetic muscle." He went on to explain how he had found Louise washed up by the river, her face and womb carved deftly away by the man who had hated her, loved her, and wanted her all at once.

Louise let them speak of her as a spectacular thing. She was quite used to it.

Lizabeth nodded, her veiled hat nodding with her. She had not removed it. She brought the tumbler to her lips, then away. "Lynch's smoky-faced angels. I see it plainly now. You do beautiful work, William." Lizabeth inclined her head. "May I have her tonight? I should like to examine her more thoroughly."

The Doctor's posture did not change, but he moved his arm to the back of the chaise, his hand curving about Louise's jawline in a way both protective and possessive. Louise leaned into him. The comforting scent of him—dust and time and raw meat—surrounded her. His fingers played over her hair and Louise felt herself want.

She wanted him. She always wanted him, a sweet, never-ending ache that filled her to her seams. "Lizabeth, why have you come?"

Lizabeth set the glass down and stood up. "I have offended you."

"I'm merely curious."

Lizabeth reached for the veil and drew it back. Her vampiric face was heart-stopping in its intensity, so finely carven and detailed she seemed less real and more like a painted statue that breathed. Louise loved her at once in a way that hurt. Lizabeth lowered her thickly lashed eyes like a demure girl. "Is it true what they say about the Poppet, William?"

"What do they say?"

"Is she your pretty one?"

The Doctor studied her carefully, his eyes as hard as crystals in the little slits in the bandages. Then he spoke, and his voice was a vibration of noise that slid up Louise's spine like a blade. "She is my wife. And yes, you may have her. But only because I trust you not to harm her."

"As if I could."

"What has been happening, Lizabeth?"

Lizabeth narrowed her eyes and raised her chin. It was obvious she was a woman very much at home in her own beauty. "You remember Dr. Andre Flamand, yes?"

It took the Doctor a moment to respond. He stiffened. That was all.

"He has been sighted here in the city not so very long ago. Your network of informants aren't terribly apt."

"They do not know about Flamand."

Lizabeth made what they call a moue in old romance novels. "Was that wisdom or foolishness on your part...Dr. Faust?"

"Both, perhaps."

"Who is Dr. Flamand?" Louise asked politely.

Lizabeth waited to see if the Doctor would respond. When he did not, she retrieved more brandy and said as she poured, "Do you understand the nature of the Elixir?"

"Some. Yes."

"The Elixir that preserves us is quite volatile, little Poppet. Many factors can affect its performance. The patient's age, for instance, or physical condition or deterioration. The list goes on." She carried the tumbler back to her seat. "Dr. Joseph Constantine Carpue is considered by many to be the father of modern plastic surgery. He began performing surgeries at St. George's Hospital in the middle of the nineteenth century. Your William and Andre Flamand were two of his first students. William was a born maestro, as you can already imagine. Andre, on the other hand, was a war doctor from a wealthy upper-class family. He delighted in such pursuits even though he did not have much talent." She paused thoughtfully. "You did not approach Andre if you wanted a statue sculpted; you only did so for an amputation. And even so, many of his patients did not survive the cauterization. But he was young and beautiful and headstrong, a picture of Oscar Wilde youth, and everyone loved and trusted him."

Lizabeth glanced at the Doctor, who nodded her on.

"But youth and beauty can only take one so far. Dr. Carpue saw no future in medicine for him. William, on the other hand, was lauded by his peers, which set Andre Flamand's teeth on edge. During one of William's more difficult surgeries, Andre even went so far as to sabotage William's work. Dr. Carpue discovered Andre's treachery and threw him out of his institute."

"After that, Flamand established his own surgery, as I recall," the Doctor offered.

"He did," Lizabeth agreed. "One of Flamand's earliest test subjects was an opera singer by the name of Pricilla Lamont, a woman whose face had been carved by the blade of a jealous suitor. But afterward, the woman was aghast at Andre's poor work. He had turned her into an even more dreadful monster." Lizabeth made a circuit of the room, glancing at photographs and fingering spines of old books. "One night she waited for him at his chateau. Andre was returning home from escorting his twin sister Natalie to the opera. He and Pricilla had a terrific row and the woman threw a bottle of formaldehyde at Andre but missed, and poor Natalie took it full in the face." She paused, letting the drama of images flutter through Louise's mind. "Andre, fully aware of his own limitations, was forced to swallow his terrible pride and begged your Dr. Faust to fix his precious sister's face, but he refused—not that I blame him in the least."

The Doctor said, "There was little to work with, even less than you, my dear." He touched Louise's hair with his delicate fingers.

"You are *quite* the talent, William," Lizabeth chastised him. "Under your knife, she would have been at least presentable to polite society—though, of course, nothing like your little Poppet here." Lizabeth took her seat, balancing her drink on her knee like a seaman, her stare directed at Louise. Her face was no longer pretty. She looked like a lioness in the tall grass, considering her prey.

"What happened to Natalie?" Louise asked.

"Andre's many terrible surgeries took their toll on the poor girl, and soon she began to die. Andre had heard of our experimental elixir and requested that William make Natalie his first test subject, but he refused. But that hardly deterred Andre. He simply stole the Elixir and administered it himself, with no real knowledge of how to use it. Andre was able to preserve the girl, but there were unforeseen side effects. The dose may have been incorrect for her."

Louise pressed herself against the Doctor's side. He threaded his long fingers through her hair. She thought to ask Lizabeth what she meant but then decided against it. She did not want to know.

Lizabeth sipped her drink. "Andre blamed William, swore vengeance on him. He promised that one day William would love someone as he loved his Natalie, and that, like Andre, William's pain would be unendurable. He would see to it."

Louise wet her dry lips with her tongue. "Why should Dr. Flamand do that?"

Lizabeth smirked. "Andre and Natalie have quite the unique relationship. Very intimate. Not unlike you and William."

The Doctor's hand clenched in her hair, almost hurting. Louise did not mind the pain.

Lizabeth turned her full attention on the Doctor. For the first time, the masklike fabric of her face showed genuine concern. "I have, of course, kept up on all your exploits, and when I learned that Andre was in the States, I decided it was time to visit." She hesitated. "*Has* it finally happened, Will? Have you fallen so far, even knowing the consequences?"

The Doctor laughed. It was not a sound he often made. It was dry and empty, the basso groan of a machine. "Flamand is a brat. You need not fear for me, dear Lizabeth. I've learned very well how to take care of myself these long years."

Lizabeth pursed her lips as if sensing some underlying meaning. "I would have visited more often, of course, except…"

"Your work. I understand." The Doctor stood up with a flourish and offered Lizabeth his hand. "No more talk of unpleasantries tonight. Please allow my servant to show you to your quarters. You are staying?"

Lizabeth stood up, giving her partner an insouciant look. "I'm quite serious about your Poppet. May I stay in her quarters tonight?" Again, she looked Louise over. "She is so very dear."

The Doctor shrugged. He did not seem unduly upset with her proposal. "The Poppet sleeps with me, Lizabeth. That is the *American* way."

Lizabeth smiled and reached for the Doctor, gliding her gloved hand fearlessly down the side of his bandaged face. "Sweet William," she grinned, "I did not say you were not *invited*."

| 11 |

Above

They met at the Café Milan on Broadway. Both of them had secrets.

In Cherry's case, that was two children. One was eight and staying with her mother in northeastern Pennsylvania. Cherry cared for her other, a toddler named Cheyenne, in an apartment she rented on Jerome Avenue. Cherry, whose real name was Cheryl Ann, was dressed in a black slip dress and a pair of red fuck-me shoes the night she met Andre Flamand. Working the streets was tough, there was no disputing that fact, but she'd made the most of it. Life had taught her, if not grace under fire, then at least survival under duress. She even wrote an anonymous blog online about the escort life, and her personal battle cry was that with prayer and determination, you can endure anything life can throw at you.

When Cheryl was fourteen years old, she bore her first child—a son named Adam—by way of her stepfather. Her mother believed in the family unit. She did not believe that the man she had married only six months earlier had been capable of doing such things to a thirteen-year-old girl and she blamed Cheryl Ann's then boyfriend for the indiscretion. Cheryl Ann did not push the point; she simply lived through the whole ordeal—the long, tiring pregnancy, the even longer (it seemed) birthing, her mother's frightening disapproval, and, finally, her nervous acceptance of her new grandson.

Adam was three months old when her stepfather resumed their relationship. Cheryl Ann's mother couldn't bring herself to believe her daughter's tales, believing instead that Cheryl Ann was damaged through and through, so Cheryl Ann went to live with her best internet friend, Poppy, in the big city. Poppy was a part-time model and full-time corporate escort. It wasn't an unduly bad existence, she explained. You made your own hours, and you could choose your own clients. Despite the movie depictions of the Evils of Prostitution that she had seen, Cheryl Ann, who was going by Cherry by that time, managed to find some pride in her work—the high-end pay, the careful filtering of clients by the company.

Then the company got stuck in some kind of business fraud, and Cherry, like Poppy, found herself out on the streets with a lease hanging over her head, her feet aching from pounding the pavement of the Cross Bronx Expressway every night, and her head on a swivel to keep the drunks and gangbangers constantly in her line of sight.

Poppy hit a rotten streak and started using meth. Her parents got her into rehab, but that was bad news for Cherry. Suddenly Poppy was gone and Cherry found herself in unfamiliar territory, too old for a pimp to take notice of her, too young to be taken seriously by anyone else. The business guru who had given her Cheyenne decided against divorce and went crawling back to his wife in Orange County, and for the first time in her life, Cherry questioned her ability to endure this hardship, particularly with Cheyenne at home, almost five now, ready to go off to school.

It seemed a hopeless situation, except that Cherry's luck seemed to be on the mend tonight.

She was sitting in her old haunt on Broadway when the manager came up to her and asked if she was looking for work. At first, she thought he meant something else, but then he explained the server they'd hired hadn't worked out, and he was short-staffed for the coming Labor Day weekend. He wondered if she had any experience. Cherry lied and said of course. Why not make a go of it? It was a nice restaurant, one of the best on the strip. It was like providence saying time to move on, Cheryl Ann. Take to make tracks. She accepted his offer on the spot and promised she'd be there first thing in the morning, 7:00 a.m. sharp.

Providence had put her in a party mood. Which is why she didn't object to the tall young man who approached her table and asked if he may join her for dinner. She figured he was a john looking for a quick score until he smiled and ordered for them both. In her experience, the johns liquored her up, but they were seldom interested in feeding her. "I can't pay for this," she admitted shyly, hiding her eyes behind the oversized menu. She'd been crying earlier and she knew they were red and swollen, not unlike her feet. "I'm in a bad spot, you see..."

"I would never expect a young lady to pay for dinner. That would be uncouth and American," he said, wrinkling up his nose. He was tall, lanky, and blonde, with nearly colorless eyes, and only the faintest shadow of a mustache on his face. He wore a red leather suit and six earrings. She pegged him for a fashion designer and thought it was possible he might be gay, except his eyes seemed to consume her, to take her apart and analyze every part of her. His accent was blandly European, not made up, a man who traveled. Cherry's heart started thudding uncomfortably under her ribs and little black dress. It seemed impossible that work and love had found her on the same night.

After dinner and three bottles of champagne, Andre escorted her by arm out of the warmth of the café and into the big black

New York night where a valet had his Aston Martin purring at the curb. Their breaths plumed together as they kissed briefly under a gooseneck lamp. Cherry made a James Bond joke and immediately regretted it. Andre thought it was quite funny and was still laughing as he escorted her to his sleek, spacey car. "I bought it for my sister, you see. She enjoys going driving and I like taking her out in style."

"You live with your sister?" Cherry asked.

"I take care of her, yes, *chérie*. She is disabled."

Beautiful, debonair, cares for his family. Andre immediately went up the ranks of her fuckable chart, if that was even possible at this point. She thought about asking Andre more about this sister, but she sensed it was a sore point with him. They drove in silence for a bit, but after a while, he glanced over, the lopsided grin on his face immediately putting her at ease. "You do know you aren't supposed to go with strange men, *chérie*? The city is dangerous."

"I'm used to it."

"You mean you do this for a living."

He must have known when he'd first spotted her in the café?

She began to worry. "Is that a deal-breaker? I'm not on drugs and I don't have any diseases. I swear." She had a vision of Andre kicking her out of his car, even tensed for it. She felt a small jab of disappointment, followed by a greater pang of regret. In that moment, Cherry wished she had been doing something respectable with her life. She wished she had waited for Andre.

Andre's voice was soft, without accent. "Do you expect payment?"

Darkness and light flickered in bright fans across the sleek black bonnet of the car. "No." She went on to explain what had happened to her tonight at the café, and how she was officially *in retirement*, as it were.

Andre was happy, that lopsided grin back on his face. "I'm glad, *chérie*. You are much too pretty for such a life. Not to mention, I would much rather we be together because we choose to be, though of course, I have the money to pay you if you need it."

She turned her head. "Are you in the scene?"

"Scene, *chérie?*"

"A designer."

"No. I am a doctor. A plastic surgeon."

That explained his extravagance, at least. He wasn't gay, just rich and flamboyant. He was, as her mother put it, a *gentleman*. It was nice to know there were still men like Andre in the world.

Cherry felt no concern, not during the long drive up the Long Island Sound, not on the snaking road that lifted them ever higher above the city and the bay. Eventually, the road turned to gravel and brush. Soon enough, Cherry felt her heart triphammering at the sight of Andre's estate. It resembled a palace, or a newly restored church, something from old Europe that belonged in the French Alps or the Black Forest of Germany. "You live here?"

"I have bought it fairly recently, yes," he said and went on to explain that the castle was designed and built by one of the madder Rockefellers in the earlier part of the eighteenth century. It was modeled after castles from Russian and German novels, with which the owner had been obsessed. A gypsy fortuneteller had warned him that he and his family were under a powerful curse. She said he would die young from benefiting so greatly from the labor and suffering of others. The only way he could lift his curse and appease the dead was to labor until the day he died.

The owner channeled that fear and challenge into his home, creating endless stairwells and hallways, even secret passages through the walls, turning his home into a virtual labyrinth. He did die young, Andre explained, falling down a long flight of stairs that his foreman had completed just the day before. The castle, sometimes referred to as The House of Stairs, changed hands many times over the next hundred years until Andre bought it for his sister Natalie, who'd become enamored with its dark long history.

Cherry shivered at Andre's story, but marveled at its architecture, the way the flagstones were fitted perfectly together like puzzle pieces, and the deep green hills that surrounded and cradled it. She saw arched, sky-high windows and ornate cornices, and even stone angels atop the battlements, eroded horns and swords held high, keeping watch over the house.

She was still gaping when the car pulled in beneath a marble canopy held up by huge, Roman-looking pillars and Andre cut the motor. She expected a full staff to greet them, the way they did in period pieces on British TV, but there was just one lone gardener working on carving the hedges. Andre passed pleasantries with him as he escorted her up the steps to the ten-foot front doors. It seemed no one, not even the help, was beneath him.

Inside, the castle looked like a castle should, full of wainscoting and buttresses and old portraiture. The air was steely with age and smelled of old books and tobacco. They made their meandering way down a cantilevered hallway full of rearing arches. Distantly, she heard the strains of scratchy music being played over what sounded like a gramophone.

She was about to ask if they were alone when a lively Bichon Frise raced down the hallway to greet them. Andre stooped to play with the dog.

So Andre liked the help and little dogs. He was almost surreal in his perfection.

"I like your house," Cherry said when Andre had rejoined her, tucking her hand back into the crook of his arm like a suitor in a Jane Austen novel. Outside, she'd made a point of catching the gardener's eye for a moment, a popular trick among the working girls to ensure a john wasn't up to something dubious. A john was less likely to abduct a girl that someone remembered. But now she saw the ridiculousness of her paranoia. She trusted Andre, his easy grace, his goofy smile. She didn't think that was even possible after her stepfather. "And your dog," she added. "I like your dog."

"She is one of my sister's companions."

"You have other pets?" Cherry had always liked dogs.

"Yes. Perhaps we'll even run into him eventually," Andre said as he guided her up and down a number of confusing and illogical staircases. She was beginning to understand why it was called The House of Stairs. "One never knows here. One can be lost for hours in this place."

Cherry laughed at that.

Eventually, he led her into what she could only call a sitting room. Cherry had her first twinge of concern once inside. It was very dark. There were high, rearing bookshelves, delicate, almost toy-like furnishings, and an enormous window covered in black drapery.

A large portrait hung over the unlit fireplace. The details were difficult to make out in the dark, but the subject seemed to be an ancestor of Andre's. He was standing poised in old-fashioned fop clothes behind a divan, a hand in his waistcoat pocket. A woman sat on the cushions of the divan, the man's free hand resting on her delicate, naked shoulder. The woman was beautiful in that old-fashioned way, delicate like bone china, with a white lily face, a moue of a mouth, and very long, dark red hair hanging about her like a bloody veil. The eyes of both subjects looked real and animate and seemed to track Cherry across the floor, but she knew that was simply a trick of eighteenth-century portrait work.

"Pretty picture," she said. "Can we put on a light?"

Andre took her coat, explaining how he was trying to keep the power bill to a manageable level.

"What about your sister? Does she mind the dark?"

"Natalie is very much at home in the dark," he explained, kicking off his shoes and padding over to a wet bar. He shed his coat as well. Beneath it, he wore a type of shirt that one sees in pirate movies and a black waistcoat that cinched his already narrow waist to a nearly waspy level. He was very thin, on the gaunt side, really, yet she found she liked it, his long, lean face and spidery fingers. He reminded her of someone from a historical novel full of war and romance and suffering.

Cherry shrugged. She was somewhat uncomfortable with the sister being here somewhere when they would likely end up doing the dirty within earshot of her...maybe even on his lovely, antique brown leather settee, she thought, glancing at it. "Will your sister notice if we make too much noise?"

Andre carried over a tumbler of expensive cognac. "Do you plan on making much noise, *chérie?*" he asked with that lopsided grin on his blonde, practically guileless face.

"I mean..." She felt herself blush, something she thought wasn't possible anymore.

Andre inclined his head graciously. "We won't disturb her. Sit."

They sat together on the leather settee in the near dark. Cherry cradled her drink, afraid to spill anything on the antique everything. They talked about her children, Andre's career in medicine, and the history of the old house. Finally, they kissed. Andre was very good at kissing. He moved his gaunt hands over her face as if he were examining her, learning her contours in the dark. If she had one complaint, it was the strong chemical odor in his hair and on his skin, the smell of hospitals, the sick and the dying. Then she reminded herself that his work was all about improving beauty.

"You said you had secrets, and you have been very brave to share them with me," Andre said, getting up and fixing himself another drink at the bar. "I shall have to reciprocate the gesture."

Here it comes, she thought with a pang of horror. He was gay, or bi-curious, or had some strange fetish she was about to learn about for the first time. No one could be as perfect as Andre. "It's something dreadful, isn't it?" she said.

"Dreadful?" Andre mused as he mixed his drink. "No, *chérie*, more of a burden. I have been granted knowledge that has changed me irrevocably. It has perpetuated me."

Oh, Christ, he was a born-again.

"Do you know the story of Faust?"

Cherry gulped her drink, her spirits sinking. "He sold his soul to the devil or something."

"He invented an amazingly simple formula that preserves human tissue exactly as it is, yet he refused to share his secret with others, forcing them to experiment with tissue samples from his patients to perfect the craft. Being unwilling to preserve my sister or me, William forced me to find the formula on my own. In so doing, I've been able to preserve myself. *Chérie*, I am immortal."

Cherry snorted her drink. Her eyes flew up to the portrait above the mantel. No wonder it looked like Andre. It *was* Andre. He had probably commissioned an artist to paint himself and his sister after the eighteenth-century style. "Like a vampire?" She'd thought guys with those types of fixations had gone out in the nineties. Apparently not.

"No, *chérie*. Vampires are dead. I live, and shall do so eternally."

It must be part of his game, his fetish, Cherry thought. Though peculiar and disappointing, she decided to play along. He looked like a good lay, damn her hormones. And she could do worse than some rich, beautiful, French doctor who thought he was the Vampire Lestat. "And your sister? Is she a vampire too?"

Will she be joining us? she wanted to ask.

"Alas, no. Natalie suffered a terrible accident in her youth, and when I perpetuated her, I misjudged the required formula. Thus, my poor dear sister is incomplete. She suffers still."

"What are you talking about?" she asked. Her nerves were on full alert finally. She turned her head to follow his quick movements in the dark. She watched him walk to a sidebar and open a black doctor's bag of the type you normally see in old movies. He removed a corked bottle and a handkerchief, and that was when Cherry decided she'd had enough.

Andre was beautiful and mysterious. Quite obviously, he was into some kind of bizarre fetish. And his house...oh god, it was like something out of a Hammer movie she'd seen as a young girl. It was all too much, frankly.

Quietly, she rose from the settee, kicked off her heels, and made a dash for the door in her stockinged feet. Andre didn't follow, thank God, but as soon as she reached the hallway, she realized the castle was like a maze. They had made their way to the sitting room through a series of interconnecting hallways and stairwells, but she couldn't be sure if they'd gone left or right. All the arched hallways looked the same, and a number of bizarre stone stairwells lead both up and down, but in no logical way she could follow.

"*Chérie?*" came Andre's voice from the doorway of the sitting room. It carried an amused lilt, as if he were mocking her, challenging her to escape. "I would not go so deeply into the house. You will get lost, and my sister's pets are afoot."

Her body trembled; her heart kicked her in her throat. She clutched her open mouth to keep from whimpering as she chose a direction at random and padded down the long, twisty hallway. It carried her this way and that, up and down shallow staircases that made no sense whatsoever. The place was a nightmare. She crept down one identical hallway after another. Arches lead off in random directions into darker spaces riddled with yet more of those damned stairwells. Some of the stairwells disappeared into walls. Others led down into even darker places. She saw no windows. She saw no doors.

As she passed one of the many stairwells, she heard a faint, low groan, a sound almost human. She badly needed to find a way out of here, and still…she backtracked and stood there, staring down a short flight of stairs that curved like a crooked spine into absolute darkness. The grunting came again, more insistent, followed by a busy, rhythmic thumping noise against the floor. Her mind reeled with possibilities. Was it someone tied up, trying to get her attention?

She gasped for breath, too afraid to run, too afraid not to. What if it was some poor girl like herself? One of Andre's other prisoners? What if she left the girl behind, alone, to suffer? Against her better judgment, Cherry padded down the cold stairs. "Hello?" she squeaked. Darkness swallowed her voice at once and she felt the little guard hairs on the back of her neck stand up.

The darkness stank of stale water, stone, and sweat. Beneath it lurked a new-penny scent she instinctively knew was blood, yet she pushed on through the dark, bumbling blindly along the damp flagstone walls, feeling with her fingers. "Hello? Is anyone there?"

Thump…thump, thumpthumpthump. The grunting sound increased, becoming more urgent. Louder. Heels beat an urgent tattoo against the floor.

"I'm here, I'm here!" Cherry cried, fishing out her cigarette lighter and spinning the butane wheel. A click later, a flame bounced up and threw a few weak feet of light ahead of her. She only saw it for a half second, no longer than a sudden glare of lightning, but it was enough to make her scream bloody hell. Turning, she stumbled away, throwing up through her nose and mouth, leaving a trail of sick behind her as she scrambled spider-like up the slick stone stairs. She slipped halfway up, cracked her jaw against a stair, and finished at a crawl.

I did not see that oh god I did not see that no god I did not see that thing doing that...

Cherry dropped to her hands and knees and screamed to heaven as another volley of vomit burst through her nose and throat. She smelled her own fear, her sick, her own urine running down her legs. That thing...what was it? What the fuck was it? It was huge, bear-like, horribly deformed, and crippled-looking, like a creature made all of different parts, wrong parts. Some parts were human and some were animal. Some parts looked inside out. Everything was wrong with it. But it had a penis. She knew that much because it had been thrusting it enthusiastically in and out of some young girl's faceless eyehole while her heels beat crazily against the floor...

No...I didn't see that...my mind made that up...that wasn't real...

Behind her, the thing bellowed in a low, pained voice. She had interrupted it. She had made it aware of her. Claws scrabbled busily against the stairs as it came. It wailed piteously. It wanted her. It wanted to do things to her...

With a roar of determination, Cherry pushed herself up. She ran like some panicked gazelle down the insanely crooked hallways. She had no sense of direction. No idea where she was going. She was screaming and sobbing in equal measure. She ran and ran until she found herself in a foyer of some kind. There was a hat tree and a credenza. She didn't see a front door, but there was a winding staircase that led up. No more stairs, she thought hysterically, please god no more stairs...

A grunt sounded from behind her, followed by heavy, trotting footfalls as the animal thing followed. It was running now, galloping, eager with interest. Stumbling, Cherry smashed into a vase on a credenza. It toppled over, the crash making the thing howl. With no choice left, she scrambled up the stairs on all fours.

The tinny music she'd heard earlier increased as she ascended. A symphony was playing, only one from another century. Music from across oceans of time. Sobbing herself sick, she rounded the top of the stairwell and spied a long, crooked hallway yawning ahead. One door lay open, with a strip of light falling upon the floorboards. God, somebody had to be here! Somebody had to help her! Whimpering, she lunged for that small bit of light, that welcoming illumination. But as soon as she reached the door, she hesitated.

It was a lady's boudoir of some kind. It was furnished with more of that delicate, doll-like furniture, and a young woman sat on a divan near the gramophone she had heard playing from down below. She was tiny like a child, a tiny child-woman in a room full of tiny, child-woman furniture. Like Andre, she was dressed like a creature from another century, and when she looked up, Cherry saw a curtain of dark, long, medusan hair concealing her face, and two mad, child-woman eyes.

"You've got to help me..." Cherry cried, stumbling in. "I have to get out of here. I have a daughter, please..."

The child-woman moved slowly, mechanically. She pushed aside her curtain of hair, and Cherry saw her face and screamed all over again.

Behind her, something stirred. Cherry felt a hot lick of breath on her neck.

As she gasped for breath to scream again, Cherry breathed in a massive gulp of nauseating, sweetish ether from the cloth cupped in Andre's spidery hand. She'd seen such things in made-for-TV movies and often wondered why the heroine didn't fight off her assailant. Finally, she learned. Andre was ridiculously powerful, and his hand clamped over her face like some alien creature. The chemical struck Cherry's brain with a hammer blow and she fell backward into Andre's waiting arms.

His dim, smiling, voracious face was the last thing she saw before the darkness stole her away. When next she came around, her life had become nightmare fabric, and Cheryl Ann came to the realization that there are some things one simply cannot endure.

***

Louise woke alone in bed. It was not an altogether uncommon occurrence. The Doctor often disappeared for hours at a time when certain medical emergencies came up, but the reappearance of Lizabeth had her concerned.

Lizabeth had been with them for two weeks. Each day on waking, Louise found the Doctor gone where once the Doctor had remained pressed against her, his scent overwhelming her as she woke from her dreamless subterranean sleep.

She sat up, dressed in a gown of gold moiré. Other gowns were scattered about the enormous, antique poster bed, gowns in peacock blues and dire greys and gay cathouse reds. The Doctor had an indelible fetish for dresses. He bought them from the most far-reaching couture shops, places in Bengal and Morocco and French Polynesia, and other places she could barely pronounce. He bought combs, hats, gloves, and shoes all in her size. Some nights he spent hours simply dressing and undressing her, finding just the right ensemble to compliment her white skin and black hair. Then he spend hours more combing her hair, twisting and pinning it into fantastic chignons, and dressing her face with cosmetics until she was begging him to just fuck her already.

The Doctor said she had no patience. He was a cruel man, and his torture relentless.

He'd never shared his fetish with anyone before, until Lizabeth. Together, the two of them had played with her most of the evening and long into the night, choosing and discarding multiple outfits before finding something they both agreed upon. Lizabeth had wanted to dress her in a kimono, her hair gathered into odango buns on both sides of her head. The Doctor had preferred a more traditional look, corset and bustle, gown and chignon, and black fencenet stockings he rolled smoothly up her legs before hooking one knee over his shoulder and taking her, plowing relentlessly into her depths with such force and fury a human woman would never have survived his love.

Later, they argued amicably over her supine body. The Doctor was fond of her lying very still as he fucked her senseless, whereas Lizabeth enjoyed watching her writhe in undulating waves of pleasure and pain as she slid a number of jewel-tipped needles under Louise's fingernails. The pain was not terrible; Lizabeth was a master at needles, ropes, and scarves. But Lizabeth was not her lover; she was not the Doctor.

At first, Lizabeth's presence had been disturbing and thrilling. It was more than lovemaking; it was art. Louise did not mind performing for her, and she did not mind sex with Lizabeth. Lizabeth was exquisite all over, and, after all, she had endured many worse encounters in years past. But as the days and nights wore on, Lizabeth grew rougher with her, dominating her, testing the limits of her pain tolerance. Not that she minded the pain, but such things belonged to the Doctor.

Louise sat on the edge of her marriage bed and mused over the possibility of killing Lizabeth, killing a Timeless. If she cut her up, burned all the pieces, would Lizabeth survive? Would some small spark live on to roost in the remnants of the body? Could it rebuild itself into its former splendor? She imagined a small, hapless creature passing through biological stages—worm and cockroach, fish and frog. Afterward, would Lizabeth seek vengeance? She might hurt the Doctor. Lizabeth might be just as powerful. She might have allies. Armies.

Louise stripped off the dress that smelled of Lizabeth's perfume and moved to stand before her dressing mirror. Hers was a taut, young body, pale white with only the slightest blush of bluish color at her breasts and groin. Her nipples were like crystals and the folds between her legs clean and smooth. There were no scars anywhere, though her eyes were not the same. Her left was blue and her right brown. The one and only time she questioned the Doctor about this, he said that they were beautiful; they were his humility bead. Her yard of blue-black hair rained down upon her as she changed into a long satin slip dress and made her way into the bedroom's anteroom.

As usual, Rachel had brought her breakfast—tea, carefully sliced blood oranges, and imported chocolate digestive biscuits, which the Doctor had gotten her helplessly addicted to. Louise unfolded the morning edition and looked for something interesting to do with her day, since it seemed the Doctor and Lizabeth were occupied with matters she was not privy to.

There was an art exhibit in SoHo, and an outside blues concern at Battery Park, but Louise craved something more detached, something she could see but still stand apart from. The new African elephant exhibit at the Bronx Zoo looked interesting.

After breakfast, she dressed in street clothes and a leather jacket and painted her face like a modern woman. Then she took to the crumbling catacomb of tunnels that she had long since memorized. She wound her casual way upward, finally emerging onto the platform for the #5 Train. The conductor was one of the Doctor's allies; he smiled and offered her an imperial bow of the head as he let her freely board.

In years past, she had been too afraid to ride the subway alone. No more. There was nothing aboard that could harm her. A knife would barely penetrate her Timeless flesh. A derailment would hardly distress her.

The ride was brief and uneventful, and soon she found herself passing through the grand, fairytale-like gates of the zoo. She showed her seasonal pass and started walking down the winding stone pathways, past family clusters and groups of children standing at concession stands. The zoo was unusually crowded today, and for a while, she feared she'd made a mistake, that the art exhibit would have been more to her taste. Then she saw the elephants down in their great stone pit, and she changed her mind immediately.

There was a young bull, his two wives, and a little one. They pranced as if they were full of air. They were pungent and alive and just lovely. Seamless and perfect, like creatures expertly modeled of clay by a brilliant artisan.

A man standing next to her said, "Elephants are the oddest things. So naked. Almost skinless."

"They're beautiful," Louise insisted. She did not like her thoughts interrupted.

She turned to look at the man who disliked elephants. He was tall and lean and dressed in a black jacket and a formal white shirt and blue jeans. His face was open and adventurous, perhaps too thin, and he had pale blue eyes and a lot of yellowish curly hair and glasses. He was strangely ugly-beautiful. He grinned at her and then reached down to lift a tiny girl so she could better see the elephants. Like him, she had a lot of yellow hair and round blue eyes that widened at her first sight of the strange beasts.

"Giovanna likes the elephants," the man announced. "I'm now officially in the minority."

"They're very strong," Louise told the man. She knew all about elephants from reading about them and other animals in the

Doctor's vast library. "Elephants are considered the strongest land animal on earth. They never forget a wrongdoing. If you lose the trust of an elephant, you may never gain it back."

"Is that why you like elephants?" the man asked.

She felt a vague surge of annoyance. "I like them because they're animals."

"And you like animals."

"Yes."

He raised his blond eyebrows. "And people?"

"People are not like elephants. I do not like people," she said.

"All people?" He sounded surprised as if she had said something absurd.

"People are stupid and ugly. Leave me alone." She walked away toward the big cat enclosure. She liked the cats almost as much as she liked the elephants. There was a big, heavy tiger with a shaggy amber coat sitting halfway up a tree in the enclosure. He looked hot and sad and she wished there was a way to free him. She imagined him running among the unwary humans in the zoo, wild and alive.

The man was back. Perhaps he was following her? "Do you like tigers too?"

"Tigers are very adaptable. They can live in the Siberian taiga, the open grasslands, or even swamps."

"Do you always talk like that? Like you're reading out of a book?"

"Do you always bother people who tell you to leave them alone?"

He gave her a lopsided grin and she felt her anger wane. "I'm Jacob."

She didn't offer her name. That would be too forward. "I like tigers too," she said instead.

"Do you like ice cream?"

She thought about that. It had been a long time. "Yes."

"I'm getting Giovanna some ice cream. Care to join me?"

She wanted to look at the tigers, but she also wanted to look at Jacob. She decided to go with Jacob and Giovanna.

Jacob bought three ice creams on sticks for them and they rested on a park bench under a tropical tree. White peacocks fluttered by, voices shrilling, feathers ruffled in the cooling autumn wind. The smell of sawdust and animal droppings was strong on the air. Louise didn't mind; it was the smell of things alive. She carefully unwrapped her ice cream and bit into the crackling chocolaty coating while Giovanna mushed hers between her fingers.

"She's only eighteen months; she doesn't *get* ice cream," Jacob told her apologetically.

Louise broke off a shard of chocolate and held it for Giovanna to nibble. Giovanna gobbled the chocolate. "Ma-ma?"

"Gio likes you," Jacob told her. "She's usually afraid of strangers."

"She's making a mess," Louise complained with a guarded smile.

"She does that. You have beautiful eyes. Heterochromia, isn't it called?"

Louise used her napkin to wipe Giovanna's face, all smeary with chocolate, while Giovanna babbled on. She ignored Jacob's compliment. "I like children too."

"Do you have children?" Jacob asked.

"No."

"I guess you want to, though."

"I can't have children," she said, looking at Jacob. The bodies of the Timeless did not function that way. They lived, but they could not *make* life.

"Sorry," he said, sounding sincere. Jacob had a mole on the left side of his neck. For some reason, she thought about touching it.

"My name is Louise," she said suddenly.

Jacob smiled. "You look like a Louise."

"What does a Louise look like?"

"Just like you."

After the ice cream was eaten, and Giovanna washed up, Jacob took them through the rest of the exhibits. They saw spider monkeys under big domes and llamas in pens and passed silently through the darkness of the reptile house. When one of the boa constrictors whipcorded past the heavy glass, Louise clutched Jacob's arm. He was very warm through his jacket. Like the animals, he smelled alive, denim and dull sweat and some faint aftershave. Then they were at the opposite gates and Louise realized the afternoon was mostly gone and felt a pang of disappointment.

She walked with Jacob out to his car, Jacob carrying Giovanna in his arms. She looked at other couples doing likewise and felt a momentary swelling of pride. A feeling of *belonging*. She was just like other women now. Here she was like them, not Timeless. No one looked at her twice. For the moment, she was alive, not some perversity brought to life past her time.

Jacob opened the back door of his Land Rover and buckled Giovanna into her baby car seat. Then he turned, almost bumping into her. "Hello," he said as if they were meeting for the first time.

Louise smiled at Jacob. She could feel the heat pouring off him. His skin was very tan, like a man who worked outside, his hair streaked by the sun. He made her feel unaccountably pale, a subterranean creature like the snakes they had seen.

"Thank you for coming with us today," he said, leaning against the door. For the first time, she noticed he didn't have a New York accent. His vowels were longish, old-worldly. "It was nice having company for a change."

"Where is Giovanna's mother?" she asked with genuine concern.

"We're not together anymore. Today was just my day with Gio. I need to drive down to the Bronx and drop her off. Then it's home for me."

"Where do you live?"

"Lancaster. The Old Order."

She thought about that. "You're Amish."

"You say it like it's a disease," Jacob laughed. "It's a long, sad story. "No twists. Not very interesting. Do you still dislike people, Louise?"

"No," she admitted. "I like Jacob and Giovanna."

He laughed at that, too. "Do you have someone waiting for you, or would you like to go with us?"

She thought about that. The Doctor would still be working with Lizbeth. Doubtless, he'd yet to realize she was gone. So she went with Jacob.

***

When Jacob returned empty-handed from the apartment complex, he looked older, less like Jacob, like a little piece of himself had gone with Giovanna. Louise sat patiently on the front seat of the Land Rover until he slid into the driver's seat. She waited while he did the ritual of buckling in, turning the engine over, resetting the brake. His eyes were far away and his heart was with Giovanna. She knew this.

She suggested a café on Maiden Lane near Broadway that she had read about in the newspaper but had yet to visit. There they had cappuccinos, cheese and cherry Danish, and chocolate donuts with a creamy glaze. Jacob had only the cappuccino. Louise ate the rest.

"How do you eat all that and stay so thin?" Jacob asked.

Louise was surprised by the question. The bodies of the Timeless were unaffected by such things. "I don't know," she said in all honesty.

"Fast metabolism," Jacob mused. "I'll need to bring my grandmother's fastnachts next time. You'd like them." He hesitated, uncertainty creeping into his eyes. "I mean, if you think there will be a next time."

Louise licked at the delicious syrupy grease on her lips and fingers. Jacob watched her lick, fascinated. "What happened to Giovanna's mother?"

Jacob wasn't unduly alarmed by her question. Perhaps he was expecting it. "Oh, well, we met online. I used to go down to the public library in Lancaster when I was younger. I learned to use the Internet there. That was my first mistake." He grinned as if he wasn't sorry at all. "Amish boys get into a lot more trouble than you can imagine. Have you seen *Breaking Amish* on TV?"

"No," she said. She didn't watch TV and she didn't know what that was.

"Oh, well. Jen and I hit it off all right. We tried to be a family, you know? But it didn't last. Giovanna was the only good thing to come of the whole affair." He considered her for a long moment. "Is there a reason you don't like people in general?"

Louise made herself blink. She had been making herself do so all afternoon. The Timeless had no need for it—they had little need to breathe, in fact—but it was important she looked acceptably human. "When I was eight, my mother ran away from home. My father started abusing me then. He used me almost every night. When I was fifteen, I ran away too and came here."

Jacob sat silent a long, steady moment, his fingers laced together on the Formica table between them. "Jesus. Your father sexually abused you?"

"Yes. He raped me most every night. He ripped my uterus to pieces so that I could never have a child."

"Jesus Christ." Jacob stared blankly at her. "Are you all right?"

"I am now."

They went back to Jacob's Land Rover and drove down to a quiet spot near the East River. It was growing dark, and the city was filling with lights and sounds. They sat watching the barges pass on the river like giant spaceships full of light and mystery. Finally, Jacob moved out from behind the wheel and slipped his arm about her waist, turning her into the shelter of his body. "I wish I could have protected you," he said intimately into her ear, and she knew what he meant.

Louise smelled the warm human scent of him. She kissed the mole on his neck. And when he turned his head, she kissed Jacob's mouth, tasting his skin and lips. She was used to the meaty raw taste of the Doctor's mouth. This was different. Virgin.

Jacob pressed himself against her and she could feel his erection pressing into her belly through his jeans. She knew that since telling him her story he would make no further advances, so she reached between their bodies and undid his jeans. She took him into her hands, and he was warm and hard and beautiful. Jacob groaned against the side of her neck and said she was amazing like the night, and that her hair was like a river of stars. She turned her hips a little so she was astride him, her rear end pressed flush against the dashboard of the jeep. Jacob moved his great, bony hands up her legs under her skirt, pushed down her dampened bikini underwear, and slipped his fingers inside her, being very gentle.

"You feel cold," he complained.

"Warm me," she answered, watching the glitter of his eyes in the failing light.

He did. It felt good to be touched by Jacob. He touched her as if she was human, not Timeless. He withdrew his fingers and tasted them. "You taste good. Like honey wine."

She ignored his compliment, took him into herself, moving her hips slickly to encase him. She milked him until he was grunting and gripping her ass to keep her in place as he thrust up and up into her velvet darkness. He quietly spent himself even as one of the barges began to toll.

She leaned down in that last moment and took his cheek flesh in her teeth. She wanted to bite, but she kissed him instead. Before she slipped out of the car, he took her wrist in his big hand and kissed it. "You are absolutely gorgeous," he said. His eyes looked huge and dark and luminescent as if he had taken a massive hit of laudanum. "I want to see you again, Louise."

She told him to meet her at the zoo in a week and then slipped silently into the night.

| 12 |

Below

William had been a foolish young surgeon. The first time Lizabeth laid eyes on him, he'd been working over a smallpox victim in a workhouse infirmary, performing a tracheotomy in a vain attempt to aid a man in breathing. It was obvious to Lizabeth that he was well beyond even the Doctor's talented ministrations.

She had admired him and hated him at once. Admired him because of his almost supernatural skill and speed with the scalpel, hated him because he reminded her of herself five years earlier, young and virgin and ready to take on the world. Like a man of the cloth, he was full of the word that was modern medicine, but she knew that soon that light would fade as he was overwhelmed by the sheer weight of the suffering, thankless humanity surrounding him.

The patient held out for twelve hours before the disease ate him alive. Afterward, William retired to the tearoom set aside for the surgeons on duty in the infirmary, poured himself a stiff drink, and saluted her.

"How can you be so pleased, sir?" she asked, stepping into the room.

William shrugged as he took a seat near the hearth. "I prolonged his life, Doctor. How is that not a victory worth celebrating?"

She was impressed. Most doctors in the workhouse hardly acknowledged her presence. None called her "Doctor" except for this pretty young man. The best she could hope for was "nurse" or "you over there." The men never acknowledged her credentials. They tolerated her only as a kind of curiosity, a diversion to keep themselves sane. She was a wealthy landowner's spoiled only child. And yet, despite the fact that she had put herself through the rigors of medical training, they considered her an uppity brat. She poured herself a bourbon; she had long since given up on tea as any kind of comfort. "But the man died."

Again, William shrugged. "We all die, Doctor. But I made him live just a little bit longer."

She turned to study this amazingly optimistic young creature. He was tall and spare like so many academics, but unlike the old gits she knew, he was also young and blond and guileless, with rather unfashionably long yellow hair and amazing blue eyes and a smooth, expressive face unmarred by the cynicism she knew would line and cleave it in only a few short years. His wandering country accent pegged him as coming from somewhere in the south of Wales. He was probably a poor farm boy who'd gone off to the big city to make something of himself. His insouciant smile was heartbreaking in its intensity.

Lizabeth decided then that she liked him a great deal more than she hated him. She also felt sorry for him. He was so princely and beautiful and new and untouched, and he projected such a light that she just knew that women everywhere would instinctively flock to him. He'd be overwhelmed by their attentions and in a family way before he ever had a chance to really *be* something.

The thought made her sad...and angry. She sat beside him, put the tumbler of bourbon on her knee, and began to speak low and intimately, telling him all her little theories about tissue rejection and life extension. As she spoke, she gauged the reaction on his face. At first, he was puzzled, then interested, and then, finally, she saw what she had been looking for. She saw the glint in his eyes that said, yes, he believed it could be done.

Lizabeth knew then that William was hers. He was her soul mate. He was the one she was meant for. She had never much cared for the company of men—at least, not in the romantic sense—but William...yes, she cared about William. She could love William, though of course, he was too much the gentleman to make forward advances on her person. If anything, he seemed unaccountably shy around the fair sex.

For William, she would do anything. They were the same. They were *one*.

She felt that way still, looking upon him now, some 168 years later. Of course, William had changed dramatically. He was still tall and lean, but now he sat hunched in his seat in the study like some terrible wretch who belonged in the pages of a gothic romance. His hair had dulled to a sunless color that was neither blond nor grey, and his skin surpassed white and had taken on a ghostly hue as if he were coated all over with a fine layer of dust. His eyes looked silver in the gaslight, and, of course, there was the terrible mask of bandages concealing the remnants of his once lovely face. William had been thirty-six years old when one of Her Majesty's officers skinned nearly his entire face in an act of bloody retribution.

William's honor as an English gentleman would not allow Officer Pymm to have his way with Lizabeth. He had concern for her, and he had been outraged that someone would mean her harm. William had paid the ultimate price for his brash act. The Elixir they had developed together had been powerful enough to save him from the severity of his wounds, but there was nothing she could do about his face. And despite his awful injuries, she could not let a light like William go out in the world.

Lizabeth stood in the doorway of William's study and watched him sit, a tumbler of brandy in one hand, and mutter theories to himself as he penned careful notes in one of his many medical journals. "No...no, that won't do at all..." he whispered, and then, in an unexpected turn of events, crushed the tumbler in his hand like a glass egg, though he hardly seemed to notice the pain or blood he had summoned. Lizabeth flinched as she stepped into the room. She was slowly coming to the realization that a century and a half of raw, never-ending agony had driven her soul mate irrevocably insane.

"William, really." She went to him and took his hand, turning it over. It shivered with glass. She plucked the larger shards loose. His blood seeped forth, unnaturally black against his ghostly grey skin.

He did not react, though he did sit up a little straighter and say, "Rachel is retrieving the new specimens. Would you be good enough to assist me today, Liz?"

Lizabeth regarded him carefully as she went about the process of binding his hand with bandages from his medic bag. "Same experiment?" she asked. Last week, after they'd seen the patients for the day, the Doctor had requested her council on a very special project. It took Lizabeth a few moments to work through the almost mind-bending concepts that William was proposing, but afterward, she was pleased and flattered that he'd wanted to include her.

It was much like the old days again. He wasn't successful, but this had not upset him unduly. He explained that he'd simply found another way to not succeed, though he would in time. William was a very patient man.

"William," she told him as she finished binding his wound. "You know the answer."

They retired to his operation theatre, which also doubled as his lab. Rachel acted as their nurse. Normally, this task would have fallen to Louise, who was becoming quite the accomplished assistant, but William did not wish to involve her in this particular research. This was for her, after all. It was his gift to her.

As he suited up and scrubbed in, he said to Rachel, "Where is Louise?"

"I believe she's gone walking, Doctor," Rachel answered without preamble.

"Where does she go?" the Doctor asked as he tied on his surgical mask.

"Into the city. She never speaks of it."

He would, of course, ask his spies. Lizabeth counted on that fact as she scrubbed in beside him. The girl was restless, wanting...that much was obvious to Lizabeth. It was not that she did not love her Doctor. But she was young and searching as Lizabeth had been once upon a time before she found her role in life.

After they were ready, Rachel rolled out the hydraulic decompression cylinder where William had been keeping the specimens in a saline solution of his own creation. The specimens had come from various medical clinics around the state, and most were in variable conditions. Inside, the capsule bore three compartments, one to hold live organs and tissue, one for the inactive specimens, and an elevated dais in the center to complete the surgery. The room was air-filtered to prevent infection, and all the surgical instruments had been sterilized. Even so, William worked quickly, using forceps to arrange the specimens on the work platform and dictating information into a microphone that hung from the ceiling.

Lizabeth assisted while Rachel retrieved specialized instruments as he requested them. She asked questions as he worked. He explained that the inactive specimens had come primarily from clinics that specialized in Intact Dilatation and Extractions, or IDXs. She asked how he had come by such rare specimens. Politics being what they were in the United States, it was becoming increasingly difficult to come by viable fetal material even from clinics that played fast and loose with the laws. He explained that he had contacts, and many people owed him many favors.

"And the live elements?" Lizabeth asked from behind her mask. The last time she had aided him in his experiments she had avoided asking such questions for fear of distracting him. But now she needed to know at all costs. There was a functioning liver, kidneys, and a fluttering, still-beating heart, all preserved in a specialized mixture that William had developed from manipulating the Elixir. It mimicked uterine fluids almost exactly, feeding just the right amount of oxygen and other nutrients into the tissue.

"I have been using piglet organs," he said. "They're much easier to come by."

"What about the partial births? Surely the organs could be revived?"

"I've found that once oxygen ceases to reach the organs, they begin to atrophy at once. They're quite useless then."

"I see. So specimens need to remain alive to stay alive."

"Essentially, yes," he answered.

"Will we be working on the brain today?"

William bent over his work of fusing the live liver into place within the cavity of the small, inactive body, a difficult task even for a skilled micro-surgeon. It was made even more hazardous by the fact that William had to work beneath the surface of the amniotic fluid. The last time Lizabeth had aided him, William had done a marvelous job of puzzling all these human shards together into a body that managed to twitch from the force of its living organs. But that body had had no brain—no head, for that manner. The IDX abortion method necessitated the removal of a fetus's head prior to its extraction from a woman's uterus. "One step at a time," he announced. He sounded old, weary. Determined.

"You do know what we're doing would be considered immoral by even the most progressive medical standards," Lizabeth announced. It wasn't that she much cared, but she was curious to see William's reaction. She was interested to know how far her young, princely doctor had fallen.

His face was stone behind his surgical mask. "Is it?"

"Even blasphemous."

"We have not murdered anyone. Quite the opposite."

"Nothing like this has ever been done before."

"Then I shall have to be the first."

"Do you believe it will work?"

"No," he immediately answered, and Lizabeth flashed back to the small, writhing body that she and the Doctor had brought to a semblance of life the day before, a body that twisted as if in mortal agony. Then it lay perfectly still, resigned to its own, inevitable fate. It had died quite some time ago. "Not today."

"Then why do it, William?" she asked in genuine concern. After the last failed experiment, William had spent hours sitting in his library, doing nothing but watching the flames dance in his hearth as rage and disappointment poured off him like an ugly miasma.

"Because I may succeed. I *will* succeed. But first, I must fail. Perhaps many times."

It was the voice—the speech—of the old William, the one she had admired so many years ago at that sad little workhouse clinic. His rate of work was phenomenal, but then, the Elixir did many unusual things to the human body—and to the human brain. In William's case, it had taken a talented surgeon and made a supernatural genius of him. In less than twenty minutes, he had most of the organs properly inserted. All had survived the procedure. In twenty more, he had succeeded in closing up the cavity and the creature was mostly whole.

As he worked on this last, Lizabeth asked the inevitable question. "Why, William? Why do this? Other than to feel like some god?" When no answer was immediately forthcoming, she added. "It's for her, isn't it?"

"No," he said as he finished up. "For us. We will feel like a family then."

The specimen lived for forty-five minutes before the organs began shutting down. Afterward, William stripped off his hospital gown, scrubbed out, and retreated to his study to listen to the surgery's recording. Lizabeth followed him in, sitting on the edge of his desk as he scribbled frantic notes into his medical ledger in his cramped, exact script.

"I think the lack of a brain is interfering with the motor functions," she suggested. "The amniotic fluid you developed from the Elixir isn't enough to support an organism. There must be a brain. A soul, if you will."

William sat back and laced his fingers together. "Perhaps." He glared across the room at the hearth as if reading all the answers there in the snapping yellow fire. "But coming across viable brain matter will be difficult."

"Not necessarily. I may be able to help."

"Are you in possession of brainstem materials?"

Lizabeth pursed her lips. "I may be able to do better than that." There were clinics in Europe where one could buy virtually anything with enough money, and Lizabeth certainly had quite a lot of that. She even knew several baby brokers, if it came down to it, and mentioned such to William.

"I am not interested in that," he said at once, glaring at her. "That would be a breach of the Hippocratic Oath."

Lizabeth laughed at him. "How virtuous," she mused. "You wish to give your 'wife' a child, just not one with a brain. Not one that can develop properly."

He gestured flippantly. "I may as well steal a child, then."

"Why don't you?"

William gave her a dark look as if she had suggested something absurd. "You. You dare speak of ethics?"

There was one tense moment when Lizabeth feared him, but then it passed. She held out bravely against her fears, and after a moment, she saw her William shed his anger in favor of his usual stony passivity. "I saved your life," she reminded him.

He laughed at that and it was a dry and disconnected noise, like a door opening after a hundred years of solitude. "You made a monster of me."

"I made you what you are, *Dr. Faust*," she barked in return. She shook her head. "You are absurd to speak of ethics to me—you of all people." Lizabeth climbed from the desk and moved to the wet bar to retrieve brandies. "You forget, William. I have visited your body farm. I understand your work almost as well as you do. This? This is a fool's errand." She brought him his drink. "It will not keep her with you if she chooses to leave."

He hunched against her words. "She is the world."

"Your world, then, is limited."

He ignored her offered drink, went back to sulking and writing. "I cannot have a continually developing mind in a child's body. The results would be unsatisfactory, at best."

William was being a ridiculous romantic. He was besotted by that girl. He wanted to give his dolly a dolly! She almost said these things, and then reconsidered them. He did not seem to be in a forgiving mood tonight. Instead, she reached out and ran her fingertips lightly along the side of his face. "You're tired, William. You need rest. And you need your bandages changed."

He sighed and sat up straighter, letting her work them off inch by grueling inch, great pieces of them sticking to the bleeding open wound that was his face. He grunted but made no mention of discomfort.

When it was done, the bandages piled alongside his notebooks, Lizabeth climbed agilely into his lap and lowered her lips to his face. She kissed him, tasting the blood on his mouth. His terrible face did not bother her; he was still her William. Her soul mate. But his body felt like stone beneath her ministrations, cold like a statue of William, not the real thing. He glared off into the fire. She reached down his body, following the line of his cravat and waistcoat, and clutched his cock through his trousers. He was soft. But after a century and a half of life, she knew ways of correcting such things.

"Don't," he said only, not looking at her.

She pressed herself against him. "You made love to me last night, William," she reminded him. All three of them had enjoyed each other in the most carnal ways possible. He was quite beyond any altruistic intentions at this point.

"Later, perhaps," he said, sounding endlessly weary. He looked down at his notes. A drop of blood rolled off his continually bleeding cheek to drip down upon the pages. "When Louise has returned."

"We don't need Louise to enjoy ourselves, William."

He turned his silvery eyes on her. There was no light there now, nothing that was remotely human. They were the eyes of Doctor Faust, genius and madman. He took her hand and removed it from his person. When she began to protest, he stood up, shaking her off himself like some ill-fitting garment he had no use for.

Lizabeth tumbled to the carpet at his feet. She knelt there, stunned. "I don't understand you." She hated the sound of her pitiful voice, the pleading quality to it. "We *loved*."

"Perhaps," the Doctor said, brushing past her and leaving her there alone to seethe and shake on the carpet, "it's time that you left, Liz."

| 13 |

Above

The movie was about a sad scullery maid who marries a prince and becomes the queen of a vast kingdom of happy people. Jacob grimaced self-consciously all the way to the credits. As they were leaving the theater together, Gio babbling happily in his arms, he said, "It was awful, wasn't it? I bet you wanted to see the slasher movie instead."

"What do you say that?" Louise asked politely as they stepped out of the darkness and into the blinding glare of the late afternoon sun. Thunderheads were clustering overhead and the sky was near chartreuse in color. Rain had turned the asphalt streets into a slick, cracked black mirror.

Jacob smiled over. "I don't know. You look like the slasher girl type. I don't mean that you would hurt anyone. Just that it would appeal to you. I mean that type of movie. You know what I mean. I'll shut up now."

Louise looked over. "I liked this movie."

As they headed for Jacob's Land Rover, he said, "What did you like about it?"

"The girl was pretty, and Gio liked the music."

Gio giggled, hearing her name, and muttered something close to "Mama."

Jacob blushed with embarrassment. "And what didn't you like about the movie?"

"The girl didn't stop her stepmother from hurting her."

Jacob thought about that. "I guess if she had stopped her there wouldn't have been much of a movie, would there?"

"You shouldn't let someone hurt you like that." Louise's voice was deeper now, darker. Hoarse. "It isn't fair!"

"You can argue life isn't fair."

"I would have stopped her."

Jacob looked at her differently, as if he had suddenly noticed a scab on her face. "Stopped the stepmother?"

They had reached the jeep. Louise went around to the passenger side while Jacob put Gio in her car seat. When they both had their seatbelts on, Jacob said, "I have to drop off Gio. Do you want to go to dinner with me or would you prefer I drive you home?"

"Can we bring Gio to dinner?"

"Jen doesn't like her out too late."

"We could tell her a story."

"I don't want Jen to worry."

"Why should she worry? You're her father."

"It's not that…"

"Doesn't she trust you?"

"Jen's very controlling."

Louise didn't argue the point, even though she thought Jacob was acting very stupid. They could tell Jen a lie, that they were stuck in traffic, or that there was an accident, and then they could spend more time with Gio.

They drove in silence over to Jen's place and Jacob went inside with Gio. He returned a few minutes later alone, looking smaller for the loss. "Jen wouldn't let me keep her. She said she wanted to give Gio a bath." He started the car and they drove into the city. "Do you still want to have dinner?"

"Have you thought about taking Gio?"

"Taking her?"

"Back to Lancaster."

"Jen would have a fit." He laughed as if he thought she wasn't being perfectly serious.

Louise pointed at a place that served fresh seafood. "There."

They pulled into a narrow parking lot. Jacob took her hand and they walked around the side of the old brownstone to the front. "You always know what you want, don't you?" Jacob said.

"What do you mean?"

"You never defer...what I mean to say is...I'm used to the women in my Ordnung letting the men make all the decisions. You're not like that, though."

The restaurant was nicer on the inside than Louise had anticipated. Dim lights and fishnets covered the walls. Clams and oysters winked ceramically from the netting on the ceiling. Instead of booths, there were long trestle tables set up so guests were forced to sit and talk with strangers. She didn't like that aspect very much and thought about leaving, but the hostess was already seeing them to their seats.

"I haven't seen one of these communal places in a while," Jacob said, looking around. "I thought they did away with them." He then turned to her. "I'm sorry if the movie disturbed you."

"Gio would like this place," Louise said, grinning up at the lacquered starfish hanging from the nets over their heads.

"Yes, I think she would." He kept watching her carefully as if she was a specimen under his emotional microscope. "You smile at the oddest times. With the elephants and with Gio."

"I like elephants and I like Gio," Louise admitted.

"It must be hard. All the things you've been through."

Louise looked at her menu. "Do you think the lobsters feel anything?"

"Beg pardon?"

"When they go into the boiling water. What do you think they feel?"

Jacob squirmed in his seat. "I'm not sure."

"They're animals. They feel."

While they waited for their server, another couple was seated across the table from them. The man was tall and slender and blond, dressed in a black leather evening suit. His companion was a thin, childish wisp of a woman with redheaded pale skin, a black cocktail dress, and dark russet hair carefully brushed into a chignon. Her makeup was carefully applied to her stern, unsmiling face. Louise watched her until she looked up. Her eyes looked painted on, no depths within them. Doll eyes. Nothing there. She and her companion both wore overcoats and long satin scarves and looked as if they had come from the theatre or the ballet.

"You don't mind?" the man asked, indicating their place.

Jacob smiled. "What would I mind?"

The man in leather bit back a smirk. He spoke with a faint, dry European accent. "You seemed to be having an intimate conversation with your lady friend about lobsters."

"Louise is afraid the lobsters feel pain when they're being boiled."

The man folded his spindly hands. "They have pain receptors. I can't imagine they don't."

Jacob laughed nervously. "If that's true, why would they do it?"

The man maintained his tight-lipped smile. "Because man needs to maintain his place in the greater hierarchy of the world. He does so by inflicting pain on lesser animals."

Jacob and the man in the leather suit started up a lively debate while Louise studied his companion. She did not say much, just nodded or murmured under her breath while the man ordered for them both. She kept her head down, not looking directly at anyone, but near the end of the meal, she said in a faint, quavering voice, "Please, may I be excused?"

"Don't be long, *chérie*," said the man. His voice was clipped and insistent.

She gathered herself and escaped to the ladies' room.

Louise waited several minutes before following the woman into the lavatory. She stood by the sinks, watching the woman wash her hands. The woman did her washing slowly and methodically. Her fingers moved rigidly over each other, and she did not look up into the great etched mirror that hung above the taps. "You're a very stupid bitch," said the woman in a low, scouring voice. "Stop looking at me." She sounded older than she looked, and her lips barely moved as she spoke.

"You should run away from him," Louise said.

"What would you know about it?"

"He's not kind."

"I belong to him."

"There are no princes, no enchantments. You will never stop being a scullery maid," Louise explained. "I could kill him for you if you like."

The woman lifted her mechanical black eyes. "Leave me alone."

"I understand," Louise answered and went back out into the restaurant.

Jacob and the strange man were debating something new when Louise returned to her seat. Something about American politics. Soon after, the bill arrived and all four of them went out into the night.

It was far colder than she expected, and the moon hung metallic and unreal over the New York Times Building. Fresh rain had washed over the streets, and dirty water frothed down the gutters.

Cabs sliced slick and bright through the puddles of the pocked asphalt. The man in black leather walked with his hand on his companion's elbow as if he didn't trust she wouldn't bolt. He and Jacob happily argued about global warming as they made their way to the parking lot. Louise hung back, walking with her head down and watching couples pass in the puddle mirrors she crossed.

Around the corner, near the curb of the street, stood a young woman in a brief red dress, five-inch stiletto heels, and a short, sad, rabbit fur jacket. Her fur was wet and she looked cold and hungry. She was smoking a cigarette and calling to a young businessman in a Maserati, but when she turned to follow the car, her eyes fell upon their little party. Immediately, she began tracking the woman who had told Louise to mind her own business in the washroom.

"Cherry," said the women, drifting away from the oily circle of a sodium streetlamp and closer to them. Walking like a long-legged crane over a pond of dirty concrete, she approached warily, eyes luminescent. "Cherry honey? Where have you been?"

Before she could drift any closer, the man in the black leather suit turned to block her passage. His nostrils flared and his jaw clenched, a clear warning sign. He didn't touch her, but the prostitute stopped dead in her tracks as if she had reached an invisible barrier. "I think," the man in leather intoned, "you are mistaken."

The woman looked confused. "But Cherry…"

"No, there is no Cherry here. You are mistaken, *mademoiselle*."

Jacob put his hand on Louise's elbow. "Do you want to get out of here?"

Louise let him guide her toward his jeep. Once they were driving again, Jacob looked over. "Those two were really something. Did you see that?"

"Yes."

"Did you like them?"

"No."

"Me neither. Really…unusual."

"He controls her. But she likes the control. Not so unusual."

Jacob looked uncomfortable. "Do you know I have no idea where you live?"

"That's because I've never told you."

Jacob laughed at that. "You're pretty unusual yourself. Do you want to go back to your place?"

"I want to go down to the river."

They returned to their spot on the docks overlooking the barges coming in. Jacob turned off the motor and slid closer to her. This time there was less fumbling. He knew her. He was comfortable.

"You need someone to warm you tonight," he said, sliding his hand past the hem of her skirt and along the scalloped edge of her garter. He pushed her down on the seat and moved atop her.

"I feel sorry for her," Louise said.

"The girl in the restaurant?"

"The girl in the movie," she answered, opening her legs to him.

He mated her with less awkwardness and more enthusiasm. They were lovers now and there was no danger. They were one and they belonged. Louise wrapped her long legs around Jacob's waist and squeezed him tight until he shouted. After he'd spent himself inside her, they sat side by side, watching the night crews unloading the barges with their monstrous cranes. Soon he slid into a kind of half trance. She waited until he was fully asleep before sliding out of the car.

| 14 |

Below

Lizabeth checked the clock on the operating theater wall. Two and a half hours had passed and the specimen was still alive.

William hovered over the incubation tank, still dressed in his bloodied hospital scrubs, studying a temperature reading. This time, on her professional advice, he had pieced together a much more viable specimen, one containing all of its most essential parts. Now that specimen—she was tempted to call it a creature, at last—was quivering with life where it hung suspended amidst the amniotic fluid. "You were right, of course," William said. "I shouldn't have doubted your wisdom, Lizabeth."

"You'll need to keep the temperature steady," she explained as she collected their surgical tools and slid them one by one into a sterilization tray. "Even a half-degree change could cause complications."

He turned to regard her. She didn't witness it, seeing how her back was to him, but she could feel his eyes piercing her through. "Forgive me."

"For what?"

"Everything. I do want you to stay. We want you to stay."

"I'll consider it, William," she answered.

After they finished sorting the lab, they retired to William's study and Rachel made them tea. Not long after, the Doctor's poppet finally returned home. She stepped into the study, wearing a small, black cocktail dress, stockings, and heels very unlike her usual garments. She took one look at Lizabeth and turned to escape to her bedchamber.

Lizabeth sipped her tea and observed the exhaustion on her friend and protégé. "William…" she began, but he cut her off too quickly.

"She is my wife," he said. He looked shrunken and beaten down as he lifted himself from his chair and followed Louise to their room. She took another sip and set the cup down in the saucer with a polite clink.

Moments later, she was back in the lab. The room was dim, the tank covered in a dark sheet. But she did not need to see the creature wriggling within to feel its presence. It insinuated itself between herself and William like a tiresome black ocean of time and regrets. She knew it was there; she could feel it pulsing, a dark spot at the back of her mind. A minute twist of the temperature control later, she was back in the study, reading over William's notes for their next experiment. They were precise and detailed, as always. She had no trouble following them.

From the bedchamber came the sounds of a great row. Glass sang and stone shattered.

"Dear me, the honeymoon is over," Lizabeth said to herself as she reached for a digestive biscuit on the platter next to the teapot.

* * *

The girl had followed Louise to the ruined church on the river.

It was late and dark and virtually lightless. The church was an isolated jigsaw of jagged debris. Jaws of glass teeth gaped where the windows had once been. The roof had partially crumbled from time and neglect. There was no moon in the dome of the polluted sky overhead, and only a sputtering security light from a barge downriver offered any respite. But Louise knew the church, knew this doorway to the Below, and didn't require much light.

She knew the girl was here long before she heard her skittering in her wobbly stilettos. She could feel her unwanted penetration. She knew she was fast approaching, panting out her fear and reluctance. The squeal of a rat clambering out of the way made the girl start, made her breath catch as if on a thorn. Louise stood near a wall, under a decaying balcony where the choir once sang. A thin pencil of light from the barges fingered through her favorite mosaic window—that of Mary holding her murdered son in her arms. But the light did not touch Louise. The light shunned her. Instead, it chose the wary street girl in her ragged animal skin coat as she darted rabbit-like through the bowels of the broken church.

Louise thought of wolves hunting in the great north, burrowing deep into the snows to pull screaming hares out by their necks. She waited until the girl was only an arm's length away and unaware of her observer before sliding up behind her and hooking a long arm around her thin, street-worn body. Louise was very tall, and not without substance. Her Timeless body was like molded iron from an age when men broke each other's skulls with maces. The girl was human. She never had a chance.

She stopped and Louise hugged her tight like a sister, the blade in her sleeve resting in the diamond between the girl's long, stork-like legs. "No, please...!" gasped the girl.

"Yes," Louise said.

"Who are you?"

"That's none of your business."

The girl wriggled, so Louise lifted her higher, so only her toes brushed the glass-littered floor. "Stop or I'll cut the womb from your body."

The girl trembled but didn't fight. "I don't know who you are...I don't care...I just want to ask you about Cherry."

"Cherry."

"The girl you were with tonight. With the hair."

"She's with him. She belongs to him."

"The man in the leather."

"Yes."

"But, Cherry...you don't understand. That isn't her."

"What do you mean?"

"Please...let me go."

Louise considered the girl's request. "If you run, I'll hunt you. I'll take you apart like a doll." She loosened her hold on the girl's birdlike body so her toes touched the floor once more.

Slowly the girl turned. Her eyes glistened as if they were made of glass, like fragments of the broken windows in the church. She said her name was Poppy. She told a story about her and Cherry. Poppy and Cherry. It was almost too good to be true. She was sick for a while, and when her parents found her, they helped her. But then she got better, and when she returned to the city, Cherry was gone. Cherry had moved out of their flat.

"I love her," Poppy said with tears in her words. "I love Cherry. I always have. I wanted to talk to her, to tell her...but now..."

Louise held her arms loosely at her sides. Her blades were still in her sleeves. "She isn't yours anymore."

"No! Cherry isn't *Cherry* anymore!"

"I don't understand."

Slowly, almost like flitting old film footage, Poppy slid to her knees, awkward in the debris, and clutched Louise's legs. She cried upon her as if she were the queen of a vast kingdom and capable of righting any wrong. "It's her face, it's Cherry's face, but it isn't her! It isn't Cherry!"

Louise had known girls like Poppy in another life. Lost and found, wandering. She had been a Poppy and she had been a Cherry. Louise knew that if the girl had been suffering a medical problem, the Doctor would have fixed it. That was what you did for people who lived in the Below.

"Let me help you," she finally said.

* * *

"You missed tea," said the Doctor from the doorway of their bedchamber. He meant dinner, but Louise had long grown accustomed to his small Briticisms.

She disrobed slowly, her back to him, hanging each garment over her shoji screen while Rachel stood nearby in the event she was needed. "I took my tea Above."

"Alone."

"I entertained company." She slid on one of the Doctor's long gowns, purchased for her long ago when the Doctor was still courting her. Rachel began buttoning her up the back. "His name is Jacob and he has a daughter named Giovanna. Giovanna is a very pretty little girl."

"I see." The Doctor's voice was course. He sounded like he was chewing on glass fragments. "Rachel, will you leave us?"

Rachel made haste to leave.

When they were finally alone, the Doctor moved forward sleekly and with a reptilian grace, and took Louse's wrist in his hand. She was not afraid. She had ceased to be afraid of him the day she learned she had been made for him. She was his wife, but she was also his daughter, his doll. She belonged to him, and the Doctor coveted her.

He was a tall man, a black shape in a long, shimmering dark dressing gown that reached his heels. He stood straight and unflinching before her, staring down at her. Had he been relaxed, he would have been as still as a breathing shadow, but he was trembling with outrage, and the air smelled faintly of blood and ozone.

She had seen him at his worst. She had seen men try to murder themselves as he casually approached them. His eyes looked dark, flecks of black flint in his bandaged face. His hold on her wrist increased, making her bones grate. He blocked the door. Behind her stood the shoji screen and her vanity table, lined with perfect bottles of perfume and vials of cosmetics. There was no escaping him now.

"You're hurting me," she said.

He released his hold on her wrist. He reached down and cupped her chin as if he were cradling a teacup. He lifted her with no effort at all off her feet. It forced her head up and cut off her windpipe, but since the Timeless only needed to breathe infrequently, it wasn't a terrible inconvenience. The angle at which he was forcing her neck hurt more. Her two hands grasped his, but it was like gripping an iron statue. Her fingernails screeked off the petrified back of his hand.

She stuttered. She couldn't have been more helpless were she a child lifted by the maniacal winds of a hurricane.

"Betrayer," he whispered and tossed her weightlessly back against the vanity mirror. The antique, three-sided mirror erupted into needling fragments of glass that speared her through the back as she collided with it. She then slid loosely to the floor. Glass bottles, jewelry, trinkets, and makeup vials spilled forth onto the floor around her.

The Doctor didn't ask if she was all right. The Timeless were always all right. That or they were dead.

He loomed over her. "Do you love him?"

Louise lay brokenly among the wreckage, staring blankly up at him. His hands were clenched into stones at his sides, and he was breathing roughly, audibly, beneath the bandages. His rings winked in the wicked lamplight as he battled to regain his composure.

"Do you love him?" he repeated. He sounded old now, and hollow, and endlessly weary.

"My monster," she said, sitting up. She nimbly pulled herself to her feet like a stringless puppet. "How ugly you are."

Her words send a visual tremor running through his long, lean body. He tried to back away, but she too had strength. She leaped at him almost weightlessly. She climbed his body like a cat up a tall, sturdy oak, and within seconds, she had her claws in him. He half turned, to shake her off, but she reached out and scratched at the bandages on his face. Her claws found their anchor and she ripped at his mask with a roar.

The bandages came off in half pieces like a bloody, broken egg. The ruin beneath showered her lips in blood, and it was bitter. Oh so bitter.

He grunted at the impact and battered her away. She landed lightly on her dancer's feet. In the fragments of the mirror lying on the floor, she saw her own face. It was surreal and bestial, all teeth and crazy, lustful black eyes like a venomous doll come to horrific life. A thousand years showed in her eyes and a thousand massacres in her smile. On the floor, a thousand Louises snarled at her, scorned and blood-flecked, battle-worn, feral.

"Louise," the Doctor said. For once, he sounded almost human.

Then she was back at him, the tremendous force of her Timeless body sending him stumbling back against a wall. It shuddered mutely and several old tintypes dropped with crunching thuds to the floor.

She reached for his naked face, and he reached for her. He caught her hands and they looked like the arthritic talons of a bird. "My monster," he hissed. "How ugly you are."

She bit his hand, the hand that had made her, fed her. Saved her. Betrayed her. Bones crackled under the brutal force of her Timeless teeth.

He roared and turned, slamming her against the wall like some dreadful insect. He slammed her again and again until the stone wall crackled like the shell of an egg, but she would not let go. Finally, he drove her into the floor and stepped on her chest as if she were some rabid wild animal, yanking his hand away. His nearly impervious flesh tore and she was briefly freckled with black blood. The taste drove her into a frenzy of fearful desire. She reached out and clawed at his legs, knocking him to the floor with her.

He was fast and could move like a nightmare. She was faster still. She skittered spider-like over his prone body until they were eye to eye. She had her knife in hand and he had his. In seconds, both flickering blades were pressed to the opposite's throat. "Betrayer," she said. "Do you love her?"

He licked his bleeding lips. "You could have told me."

"You could have asked."

"My poppet." He narrowed his eyes in his skinless face.

"My maker." She lowered her lips and bloodstained teeth.

He flinched—but she only kissed him. She kissed him with surprising tenderness. He raised one hand and knotted it in her long hair. He could have crushed her skull like an egg, and perhaps he considered the wisdom of it, but in the end, he simply held her in place while he opened his mouth to her kiss. Their tongues slid against one another like cold eels. In seconds, their blades lay forgotten on the ground.

They ripped at each other's clothing in a frenzy of greedy desire. She took him inside of herself, her body swallowing him whole. He grunted at the ungentle way she took him, used him. She was not herself, but then, this had always been within her. She was his monster, made for him, made in his image, by his monster hands. They both knew without asking that he was not offended. She was the queen to his king, not the scullery maid to his prince. He was no prince; he was a monster, and Louise knew from long, hard-won experience that you could always trust the monster to be itself. The monster required no mask of beauty to hide behind.

She moved upon him, riding him, pushing him to take her ever deeper into his darkness. Near the end, just before he spent himself, he whispered, "My darling…my little monster."

"Yes. Call me that, maker, call me that." She threw her head back and crossed her arms over her tattered bodice so that for one long second the white vial of her body flushed with color and glowed against the shivering darkness of her hair. In that second, her voice opened up and she screamed to all the gods that had driven them both into this common hell.

| 15 |

Above

It was full dark when she awoke. She didn't know, of course, this being the Below, but she felt that time had passed. He lay beside her, sleeping like the dead. The Doctor had been working odd hours, long hours, on a project he would not speak of. It both enraged and intrigued her. It made her hate and hunger for him. She wanted to sink her fingers into his skull, pull forth every drop of his red knowledge, consume it, swallow it down past her teeth and tongue, and into the empty, birth-less depths of herself. But he was alone and apart in this thing. This...experiment left him exhausted and demoralized.

In the dark, she touched his face. Her fingertips came away red and wet as if with paint. She licked away every drop before rising in the dark and dressing sleekly in a black satin slip dress and red leather jacket for the Above.

The Doctor was horrific, but he did many good things for many people. She wanted to be like that. She wanted to be worthy of him. There were bad things in their past, old sins and half-remembered iniquities. She thought about them all as she stalked down the tunnels of their home, past barred doors behind which scraped and whimpered a menagerie of lost and damaged souls. They had both done bad things to survive, but they also did good things for the people of the Below, so it all balanced out.

She went above and through the ruined loins of the church, finding herself on the banks of the East River amidst the trash and wildwood. It was still dark out, and fires made a daisy chain along the winding river. Multiple shelters made of discarded wood, cardboard, and trash bags lined the banks. One old drunk sat under a homemade teepee, drinking generic mouthwash and jerking off to a dirty magazine. He looked Louise over and held out his hand.

"I don't have anything for you," she said and started cutting a path through the overgrowth for the broken asphalt further on where the road shouldered the riverbank. There she would hail a taxi and go into the city and find Cherry. She would do a good thing. She'd gone maybe a thousand yards before she heard footsteps crunching behind her.

Ragged, filthy breathing filled her ear. A pair of grubby hands grabbed her from behind, raking over her breasts. They tried to hold her, but her body was like hard plastic. It was Timeless, immovable. She turned in the circle of her rapist's arms and raised her hand over his forehead like an angel about to bestow a midnight benediction. He looked up. He saw. Then she made a fist and drove the blade in her sleeve down through one of his rheumy eyes.

The man died on his knees, garbling curses at her. She watched him bleed out at her feet, scratching like a wounded animal at the ground.

"I said leave me alone."

One more bad thing she would need to make up for.

***

"Is this the place?" Louise politely asked, looking up at the behemoth of stone standing silent sentinel upon its high ridge. The arched and barred windows winked in an unfriendly manner, and the angels overlooking the parapets had eroded into malformed beasts.

The cabbie read the address off the GPS on his dashboard. She had gotten the address from the man in leather's wallet when she and Jacob had exited the restaurant. She was an excellent pickpocket. "You wanna go somewhere else, lady?" he asked, sensing her hesitation.

"No," she answered just as politely. "This is the place."

After tipping him, she went up to the front door. It was firmly locked, but she had expected that. She took the big doorknocker in the shape of a human hand and let it fall twice. No answer. There did not seem to be any help on the premises, or anyone moving about in the house. There were no lights, no life. She went around the side of the castle, testing windows until she found one that swung inward.

She was in a new place. The room was dark and cavernous, with cathedral ceilings and steeply arched doorways. Armless statues were poised in random places, and large, ornate stone vases filled little niches in the walls. In the room she found herself in—some kind of game room, she supposed—she saw billiards tables and card game tables. A game of senet had been left out on a lion-footed pedestal table as if the two players had gone off briefly somewhere. She ran her fingers over a frieze before making her way to two great oaken double doors and letting herself out into the loins of the castle.

Statues of coy Grecian youths lined a number of long hallways that twisted in various directions. The ceiling appeared to be painted in the Romantic style. She thought she spied what looked like gods and heroes massacring each other, but she couldn't be sure because everything was so dim. The only illumination came from some slit-like window panels set high up near the ceiling. Through a skylight, she spotted a raven pecking at the glass.

She chose a direction at random and started walking. Despite her light step, the square heels of her boots smashed against the stone floors like mallets. She passed darkened portraits of people two hundred years dead. Numerous statuettes sat in little nooks, mostly angels with upraised wings. Ahead, she spotted a dim light. She walked toward it. She was concerned, but not afraid. She had seen much more darkness Below.

She found herself at the foot of a long, spiral stairwell and began to climb. It led to a new but equally identical corridor. Ahead, she heard music playing, ancient and tinny. Someone was rounding a bend and now stood at the far end of the dimly lit hallway—a figure, small, slim, another darkness in the tunnel with her. They regarded each other carefully. When she resumed her steps, the figure mimicked her. When she stopped, it stopped

Eventually, the two of them halved the distance between them, like two mirror sisters. Now, she could see the figure was the girl with the doll eyes. She was wearing a long, old-fashioned gown, high-necked and frothing with antique lace that seemed to envelop her emaciated little body. Her shoes were like Louise's when she was Below. Old. Outdated. Her hair was down and dark crimson and very long like a wash of blood spewing from the back of her brain. It fell in a dark veil over her face and chin so only her doll eyes shone forth like two little abysses.

Louise took the final few steps. The girl stayed where she was. "Natalie," said Louise.

"You've come at last," said the girl. Her voice was that coarse, grating sound, unpleasant in every way to the senses like a woman who had been locked behind doors and screaming for days. It made Louise want to clear her throat. "How did you know?"

"Lizabeth," Louise offered. "She said Flamand was hunting us. *Me*."

"But..."

"I'm not offended."

"You should be."

"You are like me. We are the same. Timeless."

Natalie's eyes widened slightly behind her mask of hair. "You should go."

"I don't want to go. I want to stay. I want to know."

"Know?"

"Your story."

"Brother will be back soon."

"Yes."

"He will be back and he will hurt you, Poppet."

"Yes."

"He will hurt you for *me*."

Louise reached out and touched Natalie's hair. It felt dry and brittle and dead. Natalie jerked back. "He'll be back soon, sister, and you do not know my brother. He is a monster."

"Yes," answered Louise. "I know all about monsters, sister."

| 16 |

Below

Roaring, William threw his journals and notebooks against the far wall, then scooped up the trays of sterilized surgical instruments and threw them to the floor. Unsatisfied, he grabbed up the wheeled car they kept the trays on, lifted it effortlessly above his head, and tossed it at the incubation tank. The tank exploded as if a bomb had gone off, and yellowish fluid sloshed to the floor, soaking his carefully penned notes, soaking everything in its path until he stood ankle-deep in the stinking miasma of his own worthless experiment.

Lizabeth stood near the bookshelves, back to the wall, arms clutching the stone surface as if she had been crucified upon it. She shuddered as the palatable waves of William's anger struck her again and again with hammer blows. "William..." she kept saying as he went about the machine-like task of destroying his lab, "William, for the love of God..." She looked around, hoping for some assistance, or some way to control him, but what could be done? What force, aside from that damned girl, could harness his rage? She was alone. Rachel, at least, had had brains enough to exit the room the moment William had discovered the specimen dead in its tank.

The others in the Below gave Dr. Faust a wide berth as a matter of course.

Lizabeth was alone with this raging monster, with her abomination...

"William!" she cried as he stood there, trembling like a black mountain, ready to toss a gurney into a wall.

He slammed it down in response, metal parts twisting like toys. He was breathing like a locomotive behind the bandages, and his body shook as if he were conducting a powerful electrical charge. The atmosphere around them thudded with maniacal rage. Torn electrical cables hung from the walls, spitting like snakes. There were pocks in the stone floor and walls, and glass debris lay glistening everywhere like some terrible gauntlet. In all her years, she had never seen him like this, so completely out of control.

He leaned over the gurney, fingers twisting the metal yet more, and let out a noise that Dr. Faust should never, ever make. It was a thousand times worse than anything she had heard from his secret gallery, the place where he harvested all his living parts. A mournful screech rose from deep within the body farm as some pitiful half-creature responded to the miserable sound his master was making. Farther on, out in Above somewhere, a dog let out a single trembling bay.

Lizabeth clutched her mouth. She regretted what she had done. What she had felt. She had never meant to do this thing to him. Not to him. Not to her William. Compelled, she strode forward to put her hand on his shoulder. She would confess. She would make it right. "Will...oh, Will..." she began because that was what he was to her.

William. Will. The man she loved, and who loved her. The man who would no more harm her than he would his precious Poppet.

He was hers. He was her monster. She had *made* him...

He rounded on her blindly, eyes silvery and feral. They were the eyes of Dr. Faust, not the eyes of William. They were the eyes of the mad and the damned.

She shirked, but he was too quick. He grabbed her by the arm. His grip was like a machine with hydraulic strength. The pressure was unbelievable. With a grunt, he tossed her head over heels the length of the theater as if she were a doll made of feathers and air and thread. It happened too quickly; she had no time to react.

Lizabeth hit the stones of the far wall with a wet crackling sound. Her head twisted to one side and she felt her neck snap in two places. She crumpled, insect-like and defeated, to the floor and knew only darkness for some long while.

| 17 |

Above

Louise followed Natalie into her boudoir. Petite Queen Anne furnishings were scattered about, with a large window seat that looked out over the misty Long Island Sound. There were antique urns in little alcoves, and huge portraits of ancient places in exquisite oils dating back centuries on the walls. Rusted candelabra hung from the ceiling, and billowy white curtains from the windows. Natalie went to the antique gramophone and lifted the needle. Were it not for the view, the room would have looked like something from another time in a far-off kingdom.

"I like music," Natalie explained, walking to two opposing divans with a small tea table and samovar stacked between them. "At times, it is my only companion. That and my pets." A white dog barked from her vast antique sleigh bed and followed Natalie to one of the divans. She indicated the other and Louise graciously accepted it.

She poured them both tea as if she had done so a thousand times before.

"You have no servants here?" Louise inquired, petting the little dog as it begged for biscuits beneath the table.

"No one will work here. I do most of the work." Natalie looked up through her mask of hair. It pooled around her on the cushions, dry and fiery. It looked ready to break, though Louise knew it would not. Despite its appearance, it was invulnerable to such things. "I'm stronger than I look."

"You are Timeless."

Natalie laughed at that, a grating noise that scraped Louise's bones. "Yes, we are that."

The tea was good, lemony, and sweet.

Slowly, Natalie lowered her head. "Brother has gone into the city. He will be back soon."

"Flamand."

"If he catches you, he will kill you."

"But he has to catch me first."

"You don't know him. How strong he is. He will do anything to fix me."

Louise set her teacup down. "Show me."

"You don't want to see."

"Show me."

Natalie sat back. Slowly, very slowly, she lifted the veil of her hair. The Cherry face stitched there already bore cankers and ulcerations. Louise knew enough about medicine to know Natalie's Timeless body was rejecting the graft. Their bodies did not react well to tampering or alterations. They were made perpetual at the time of their creation. "Do you see why I never go out into the city as I am?"

Louise had seen many horrors in her time, but not many compared to Natalie's sad monster face. The Doctor was terrible to look upon, it was true, but even so, his face was a bloody open wound. It was not this rotting *thing*...

"I'm sorry," Louise said, sipping her tea.

"It's much worse than that." Natalie's voice was low and scorching. Louise had to strain to hear every word. "He brings girls home. He takes their faces. He puts me in such pain. You don't know." She bowed her head. "He's embarrassed by me."

"Why don't you kill him?"

Natalie clasped her two small, glove-like hands together. "He's whole…and Timeless. He's stronger than I am. If I try to run away, he finds me. He hunts me down. Then he does even worse things to me. There is no escaping him."

"Does he rape you?"

Natalie flinched. "Sometimes, when I'm whole. But only when I'm whole. I am his."

A door slammed somewhere in the depths of the castle and Natalie stiffened. Suddenly she became very agitated. With some effort, she climbed to her feet. She moved like the chronically ill. "I told you to go. I told you he would return."

Louise stood up. She now knew her mission. She would protect Natalie. She would avenge Cherry. She would do these things because that was what the Doctor would do. That was what the Doctor would expect her to do. "I'm not afraid," she said, releasing the crown of blades in her sleeve. She could hear the pound of feet on the stairs as *he* approached. She was very good with her knives, and very accurate. She turned toward the doorway where she knew *he* would come.

Dr. Flamand. The Doctor's adversary. Her enemy.

"Natalie?" called a dry, reedy voice, drawing nearer. It sounded demandingly angry. *"Natalie…!"*

Louise heard a benign step behind her. She smelled Natalie's rot quite plainly now. It quickly enveloped her, but before she could turn around, Natalie had her. Her long hair was about Louise's throat like a garrote, and her small, breakable-looking body was lifting her up off her feet. Natalie's strength was absurd. But then, Natalie was very old. Older than Louise. She was impressed, and, too late, she remembered what Natalie had said. *I'm stronger than I look.*

She whimpered and tried to strike backward with her knives, but her hand had no strength as Natalie tightened her garrote of hair. Instead, the knives slipped harmlessly from her grip and dropped to the floor. Louise gargled out a plea, not unlike the man she had killed on the riverbank, but Natalie was similarly disinclined to listen.

"Oh, sister mine, what a silly, naïve little bitch you are," Natalie hissed in her ear. Her breath tasted of flayed, soured meat. She tightened her garrote further and Louise's world went black in the seconds after she recognized the smirking form of Dr. Andre Flamand stepping through the door.

***

Normally, the trip from Lancaster to New York took Jacob three hours of drive time. He only went on Sundays, when the family didn't work the farm. He left before church and was back just before dark for evening services. His family was generally unhappy with the arrangement. They said he didn't walk close enough with God and that he had an English devil in him. They were probably right.

Only his father supported his decision, and only because it was best for the family farm. He couldn't hare off and see Gio anytime he wanted. His family was relatively small by his Ordnung's standards—three brothers and two sisters—and they needed every pair of working hands they could get during the hard months. That left only Sundays, the day his people rested.

As a young man during his *Rumspringa*—the "running around time" that all Amish young people experienced—he had made his fair share of mistakes, there was no disputing that fact, but he never considered Giovanna a mistake. Giovanna was his world. His family, though they hadn't entirely forgiven him for his indiscretion, at least understood the bonds of family. They knew his time with Gio was precious and limited. They did not approve of his visits to the city, but they did make allowances.

Every Sunday he was up before first light, even before the women were up, and he went down to the winter barn where he kept the jeep in storage. The jeep—like Gio—was a reminder of the English world, but Jacob's family had come to tolerate it. They had not yet met Gio, though he hoped to rectify that oversight one of these days.

Take her, as Louise had said. Yes. It would be so easy.

During the drive into the city, Jacob thought about Louise. She was a delicious mystery. There was an old-world charm about her, as if she'd sprung from another time, another place long forgotten by the modern English in their cities of soulless glass and broken concrete. She was of it, but apart from it, not unlike himself. But could he trust her? He knew he wanted to, and he thought it was in her to be kind.

For once, there was little traffic and he reached the city as the sun was first peaking. He picked up Gio from Jen, but his girl was still sleepy. Jacob put her into her car seat and buckled her tight. He started to drive.

Louise. Their times down by the river were becoming increasingly precious to him. He liked the sex, of course, but it was more than that. Louise was a drug, sweetly corruptible, and he didn't mind the addiction.

Before he even realized it, he'd driven to the edge of the East River, the south bank that had been under urban renewal for years but never seemed to get any better. The black, snaking river was hemmed in with homeless hovels. He saw laundry lines and tin barrel bonfires. Rearing above it all were the bones of the Church of St. Bridget, standing like a half-demolished sentinel as the sun slowly rose behind its weathered spire. Light spilled around it, enflaming windows full of tortured and dying saints.

He drove slowly, watching the calcified faces and hooded eyes of the homeless as he passed. A woman was climbing up the embankment of the river to the street several hundred yards away. In the pre-dawn darkness, he couldn't make out her face, but he saw that she was tall and slender and dressed in a leather coat. Her long hair shushed around her and made him think of Louise.

Yes, yes. It was she. It was Louise. So she did live here somewhere.

He watched her hail a passing cab. He was a little disappointed to learn she was one of the homeless and then chastised himself for his un-Christian thoughts. She was still his Louise, though she was certainly too embarrassed to tell him the truth. She slid inside the cab, and then the cab took off soundlessly into the hills of the city.

He felt his soul sink. Was it all worse than that? Was she also a prostitute? Putting his car back in gear, he decided to follow.

The drive up Long Island was long, tense, and tiring, but he was determined to know the truth. With Jen, he had known almost nothing. It was not a mistake he would make twice.

Gio was still asleep when they pulled up the long, winding gravel road to the castle high above. They were only halfway up the mountain when Jacob spied the cab passing them going the other way. Not knowing what else to do, Jacob parked the car at the bottom of the drive and checked on Gio. She was gurgling in her sleep. He got out to stretch his legs and followed the gravel path until he reached the turnaround in front of the castle. He wondered what he should do.

It was obvious to him that Louise led a secret life she had not bothered to mention to him. But then, what *had* she mentioned? He knew almost nothing about her. He didn't know where she had been born, where she had grown up, or what she did for a living. He didn't even know her last name.

Thoughts settled heavily upon him and made his shoulders slump as he returned to the car to sit and think. "Da-da," said Gio from the back seat.

"Dada is here," he told Gio, giving his daughter her favorite stuffed Elmo toy.

He knew he had to make a choice. Louise had secrets. Secrets led to trouble, and that was something he did not need, not after Jen, not after the way he had disgraced his family and Ordnung. He had to let this go.

With a sigh, he started the car and put it into drive. Gio wanted to see the zoo again. They would go look at the animals and eat ice cream. They would be a family, and then Jacob would take her home. He'd fight with Jen, say goodbye to Gio, and turn his back on these English ways once and for all. He'd become what he was always meant to be.

He was almost down the mountain when he made a decision that would impact the rest of his life—his and Gio's. Punching the steering wheel, he jerked the wheel and started driving back up the road toward the castle.

***

Louise glided in and out of unconsciousness. She felt that she was floating on dark water in the middle of the night on the ocean all alone. Sometimes, the darkness parted and she could make out figures, light, and snippets of speech. She was rocked back and forth as waves of light assaulted her, biting her senses with small, sharp, devilish teeth. She knew that Flamand and Natalie had taken her, and she knew that Flamand was carrying her somewhere as he talked about the surgery. She didn't understand that; there were no surgeries planned for the day. Then she sank once more beneath a dark wave and could only sleep and wait to rise again.

Eventually, the darkness broke like a black shell and she felt herself moan through numb lips. She was lying very still and there was a blinding halo of light above her. She was in an operating theater of some kind similar to what the Doctor used, but she couldn't move at all. Her body was like a stone statue, lifeless, solid, immovable. At last, she had become the dead thing she was always meant to be. For the first time in too long, it frightened her and she whimpered in desperation.

"She's awake," rasped Natalie's voice. "Brother...she's awake!"

"Yes, I see that."

"She shouldn't be awake!"

"I can't prevent it. You know how our bodies are."

Louise blinked. Her vision was blurred and dreamlike, but she could make out shadow figures moving back and forth within the halo of light. She knew then where she was. She was on a hospital gurney in Andre Flamand's operation theatre, and she was cold and dead, and yet somehow lived. Andre and Natalie Flamand stood over her, speaking softly to one another as if she could not hear them. Both of them wore hospital scrubs and green masks hid their faces.

"She is very beautiful," Natalie said softly from behind her mask. "Exquisite. Not even a scar." Natalie was touching her face, her naked, leaden body, admiring her, lusting for her, yet she felt nothing.

"Faust does excellent work."

"I wish..."

"Don't. Don't wish. This will work."

"You always say that, Brother. It never works."

"She is not like the others. She is like *us, chérie*. She is eternal." Flamand took Natalie's hands, making a bridge across the gurney, and leaned down to press a kiss to her masked lips. "A fount of never-ending material."

Louise moaned again.

"Quiet, little beauty," Flamand said, touching her cheek with his gloved fingertips. "You are afraid? Yes. Yes, I know you are. You cannot move and you wonder where you are. I shall tell you." His eyes simmered and shone as he explained. "This is my lab, at the bottom of the house. This is where I work. I have broken your neck, but you will not die. You will *never* die. Still, your body will not move until you are whole once more. It is the most efficient way to bind an immortal, I've found."

Louise could feel nothing below her chin. She tried to suck in a breath and could not. She wasn't breathing at all. She wasn't doing anything...

"You have a very special destiny, pretty Poppet." Flamand reached for something on an instrument gurney and then turned back. It was a black marker. Smoothing her face, he began drawing broken line marks at her hairline. "Because of you, my Natalie will be forever beautiful. Forever whole."

Her eyes darted and fluttered in panic. The realization made her whimper, but she could find no breath to complete the sounds she was making. She couldn't so much as even blink.

After he had finished marking her face, Andre Flamand asked his sister to hand him a scalpel. It flashed like quicksilver in his gloved hand. Louise followed the arc of its light; she was incapable of looking away.

Flamand touched her head like a priest bestowing a special benediction. "I apologize in advance for the pain, pretty Poppet. Because of our unique makeup, anesthetic is quite impossible for our bodies to metabolize, but I hope you will take some small comfort in the fact that you are being very generous in your contribution. Because of you, my beautiful Natalie can walk these city streets once more. Shall we begin, then?"

| 18 |

Below

The Doctor set her down on a gurney, Lizabeth's head lolling brokenly on her crooked stalk neck. It was canted to one side so she couldn't properly see him. She could only see him from the corner of her eye—a liquidy darkness that hovered dreamlike in her peripheral vision. She wanted to move, she *willed* her body to move, but a broken neck was enough to keep one of their immortal kind incapacitated. Lizabeth knew because she had experimented extensively with the method over the years.

"It was you," he boomed over her supine and helpless body. "You did it. Why?"

She moaned in response. Her eyes fluttered in a plea.

"Not until you tell me, Liz."

She moaned louder.

He grabbed her chin, pinching it harshly in two fingers, and twisted her head to look at him. The pain made her scream inside her own head, though she could utter no proper sound. The crackle of her own broken bones made her feel ill, but at least now she was looking at his muffled, bandaged face, his blade-like eyes—though somehow that was worse. She saw no William in those eyes. Where had he gone?

"Was it because of her? Because of Louise?" Dr. Faust demanded to know. "One blink for yes. Two for no."

Blink.

"Oh, Liz." His voice was full of seething pity. Somehow, that was a hundred times worse than his rage. "And Flamand. You know him. You've made a deal with him, yes?"

Blink, blink.

"Forgive me, my dear, if I don't believe you."

Blink, blink. Her eyes watered with un-sheddable tears.

He reached down with his large, sensitive surgeon's hands and grasped her chin. A few deft snaps later, pain and strength surged down her body. The pain made her want to heave. His anger made her want to scream. "Oh, William...I'm sorry, William..." She started grabbing at the front of him, but he pushed her down, held her there against the surface of the gurney. He was no stronger than she was—than any of the immortals were, really—yet he held her immobile with his anger as well as his brute force. "I didn't want you wasting yourself!"

"Wasting?" The word was little more than a bass growl like some old machine turning over for the first time in a hundred years.

"On her!" Liz screamed in unadulterated rage. Pain and outrage poured from every corner of her trembling, perpetual body. "Will, she isn't worthy...she isn't *us*..."

"How dare you."

His voice sounded like stones grating together. The low, thunderous sound of it froze Lizbeth dead. He knew then. He knew everything. He took her by the throat. He was surprisingly gentle until he pinched her windpipe closed.

Her fear turned to outrage. "She betrayed you!" she choked out.

"And I betrayed her first." He had the power to sever her neck. He could tear her head and spine from her body if he wanted. She had no doubts about that. Terrified, she admitted, "He has her. Andre has her. If you kill me, you'll never find her!"

He gently lifted her head and then slammed it cruelly against the surface of the gurney. "Where is she, Liz? Where did that brat take my wife?"

"Please..." she gasped. "Please, I'm *sorry*." She kept saying those words, over and over, but he only increased the pressure about her throat. She knew he would do it. He would extract her head from her body and bury her in a box in a shallow grave for a thousand years, until she went mad, as mad as he was...

She told him everything in a frenzy of fear and rage. Where Flamand was living, where he was working. She explained that they had no formal arrangement, she and Flamand. She had even *warned* William about him—back in the beginning. "Please, Will, for the love of God..." she wept, scrabbling at his stony fingers.

She had made a dreadful mistake, she now realized. She'd thought this was William. She'd thought some part of William had survived within Dr. Faust. But she'd been mistaken. The girl had taken it. The girl had taken *him*...

"Thank you, Liz," Faust said. His voice grated, sounding like it was full of broken glass. There was no William there. There was no anyone there. "We will continue this discussion once I return."

With a deft snap, he re-broke her neck.

| 19 |

Above

Jacob tested window after window until he found a pair that swung inward. What are you doing? he asked himself as he crawled inside an enormous ballroom in this impossible castle in the hills. He glared, wide-eyed, at his surroundings. Unlit candelabra lined the walls. The walls themselves were painted with frescoes of some kind of bizarre Grecian orgy. Men mounted swine and women mated with wild-eyed man-bulls.

Suppressing a shudder, he let himself out into a long, arched hallway. Doors lined both walls, but no one seemed to be about.

As he walked, he realized the mazelike corridors twisted and turned at weird intervals. There seemed no rhyme or reason to the place. Sometimes, he encountered stairwells, but they only led to more corridors, and, in one instance, ramped up and away to a blank wall. The architect must have been insane. He was about to double back, convinced he had made a mistake when he heard what sounded like the clack of hooves against the parquet floor, followed by a bellow of air as if some giant had exhaled. It made him think of one of the farm animals when it was peeved.

"Hello...?" he said, feeling stupid. At this point, some wild animal wandering the halls wouldn't have surprised him in the least. But for the life of him, he couldn't understand why he was talking to it.

There was another loud snort, sick and phlegmy, followed by what sounded like mumbled human words. It was coming from the corridor behind him.

"Is someone there?" he asked, turning.

More garbled words drifted to him. He couldn't make them out, but their cadence was almost human and reminded him of someone in pain. He was tempted to follow the sound, if for no other reason than to try and help whatever poor creature was trapped here in this labyrinth, but a spike of concern kept him sealed him to the floor.

"Help?" something asked from the shadows. He saw a pair of watery eyes. And then something else asked, "Kill?"

The hair on his scalp wriggled. The air felt electrified with danger. He couldn't explain it, but he didn't want to help. He didn't want to be here any longer. He took off in the opposite direction, following the crazy spirals of corridors and stairwells. He was going down now, deeper into the bowels of the castle, and he did not care, so long as he was away from whatever unseen thing was in the corridor with him.

"Louise?" he called, feeling every nerve grate within him. His voice echoed hollowly against the slightly askew walls. First, he trotted, then he ran. "Louise, where are you?" He heard the note of panic creeping into his voice, the lilt that warned he was near hysterics. Behind him, the hooves ticked and tapped against the floor, keeping pace with him.

Eventually, he came to a pair of swinging doors of the kind you find in hospitals and emergency rooms. The little hairs on his arms were standing straight up and brushing the sleeves of his coat. He smelled something vast and cold and reptilian. He knew it was his own fear. He knew there was something terrible going on in the room ahead, something unspeakable. *Leave*, he told himself. *Get in the car and drive away.* He didn't owe Louise anything. He'd best leave her to her world, her woes...

Yet he couldn't bear to turn around and feel his way back in the dark. Something was here with him, something he couldn't see. Something that could see him. He could only go forward.

He tested the doors and found them well-oiled and soundless. Stepping through, he saw he was in a vast operation theatre filled with light, tiled in white, and furnished with elaborate stainless steel hospital equipment. The transition from an archaic castle to a sleek, ergonomic hospital was so startling that it stopped him dead in his tracks.

Louise was lying naked on a hospital gurney with a tall man in scrubs standing over her slender white body. He was using a series of delicate instruments to tent the skin on the left side of her face. On a second gurney lay the body of a young woman. It was the woman from the restaurant, the one with the red long hair. This woman had no face at all. Only a gaping red darkness where her face should have been. Yet the woman's mangled lips were moving. She was saying, "Andre...this is taking too long," while her eyes skittered whitely back and forth in the skinned ruins of her face.

The sight made Jacob's stomach lurch. He swallowed hard against the volley of vomit in his throat.

The man in scrubs swore and released the tent of skin. His hands were bloody and slick, and Louise mewled as that portion of her face snapped back, peeled like the skin of some bloody fruit. Her eyes were wide and glaring with agony. She was awake, he saw, fully aware of everything that was happening to her, but helpless to stop it, to even scream...

"You," said the man in a low, throaty growl as he turned, scalpel in hand. "What are you doing here?"

Jacob clutched his mouth to keep from heaving. He backed up until he smashed into a hospital tray. Instruments clashed to the ceramic floor around him, the sound so great he winced. He thought about rushing the man with the scalpel, saving Louise, but his expression, as much as the blade in his hand, prevented him. His eyes were dead and full of darkness. Years of cruelty. Years of *this*. There was Gio to think about, his family. He had to get out. He had to survive. Jacob turned and stumbled through the doors and out into the hallway. It yawned ahead of him like a dark funnel into nothing. He didn't know if it was empty, or if it contained a thousand horrors. Such things no longer mattered. He pounded down the length of it, took a turn, then another.

Jesus Fucking Christ, he thought, using an English expression he never thought he would. Jesus Sweet Fucking Christ. All the corridors looked the same, and there were no windows to shed much light. Behind him clocked slow but steady footsteps. His pursuer was in no rush.

Ahead, a stairwell loomed, twisting upward. Laughing with hysterical fear, he scrambled up but found himself in yet another collection of mazelike corridors. He ran and ran until he thought his heart would burst. Eventually, he skidded to the floor on his knees. It was almost a blessing. He leaned over and tried to catch his breath. Behind him, he heard the doctor in bloody scrubs casually climbing the stairs. The doctor said in a perfectly reasonable voice, "Did he send you, *monsieur*? Are you his disciple?"

"W-who?" Jacob sobbed out.

"Dr. Faust. Did he send you, child?" said the doctor. He had reached the top of the stairs. Only the corridor now separated them. He was carrying his scalpel in one gloved hand. It winked with a nauseatingly bright, mirror-like luster.

Jacob lurched back to his feet in the hallway, glancing around for something he could use to defend himself. There were several statuettes in little alcoves, but they looked too heavy to be effective weapons. "I have no idea who that is!" he screamed.

"If that were true, you wouldn't be here," mumbled the doctor from behind his mask.

"You're fucking crazy!" he shouted. The corridor, he now saw, dead-ended in a mockingly short stairwell that let up to a large, arched window with heavy black bars. He rushed up the stairs to the window. From here, he could see his car through the hazy, unwashed glass. Gio. He had to get out of this hellhole and back to Gio!

Summoning every bit of remaining courage, Jacob turned and rushed the doctor with a shout. He was strong from working his father's fields; he thought it was possible he could make it past with little injury. But the doctor simply sidestepped him. Jacob skidded at the top of the stairwell, doing a dance of air and terror, and soon after began the long, winding fall to the floor below.

His body jounced and rolled. Each impact was like a hammer blow to his bones. The ceiling wheeled, full of angry painted angels casting out demons. He landed like a dead thing on his back at the foot of the staircase, staring up at the faceless girl from the operation theater.

He laughed at that. She looked like a demon, like something spat up from the hell his family had warned him about. "No...God, no, please...I have a daughter," Jacob begged.

The faceless girl's eyes blinked in the ruins of her face. He heard the creak of meat tearing around her tattered lips as she forced her lips into a bow of a smile. She was strangely fascinating, this human medusa of long hair and raw meat. "Such a human waste," she said, and it was the last thing Jacob heard before she reached for him.

***

Perhaps, she thought wistfully, had she the ability to scream, she might be able to endure the escalating waves of relentless red pain. But Flamand, in his cruelty, had taken even that from her. She could not escape it, could not even let it out in some petty, verbal way. Released, it might have been tolerable. But imprisoned in her body as she was, unable to react, all she could do was scream endlessly inside her own brain while he used his steel instruments to scrape the skin and meat off her face.

I am the Doctor, she thought in some floating hysteria of agony. I am him. I am my maker. At last…

If only…if only…Flamand was talented. She might have even admired his handiwork. But he was no doctor. He was a butcher. And she was his cattle.

Pain…and pain. Red-rimmed. Un-scream-able. All she could make were these pathetic little whimpers, like the sounds of some crippled kitten left in the gutter to drown in the filth of its own excrement. Again, this city was using her, breaking her, taking every living, bleeding part of her…

Doctor…oh, Doctor…oh, monster, come for me…save me…save meeeee…

She shrieked one last, long time inside the hellish domain of her own skull, and then all was blessed silence. Her body had given out, given itself over to the beautiful darkness. She wanted to be dead. She wanted to not exist at all. But she was denied even that.

She had never been worthy. She had never been anything but refuse in this city…

Blinding light and searing agony greeted her when next she woke. Her mouth stretched wide in response so she thought her jaw must break. She was lying on a pallet in a cell somewhere dank and forgotten. Pain beat at her. It bore crimson wings laced with knife edges. She could move now, she discovered. Her head, her body. She was whole once more. Her body had healed itself as best it could. It had righted her broken neck, though her face would take some time. As a result, she could feel everything. She could scream, and she did. She screamed until she vomited—and then she screamed some more.

Later, much later, when her voice had finally given out and she had fallen to the concrete floor, Louise dragged herself into a far corner of the room. It was a low, dimply-lit cellar-type space of indecipherable magnitude, with a giant behemoth of an incinerator hissing in one lone corner. So this was the final resting place for Flamand's girls, she thought. This place of the dead.

Maybe, she thought, I am the dead. Please, let me be one of the dead. The pain was suffocating and unendurable. It chipped at her mind, it ate at her sanity, but somehow, through the red-filled haze that surrounded her, she managed to breathe, and even cry a little, dry and empty.

She prayed to die, and then she cursed. Time wore on; it had no meaning for her any longer.

Eventually, a door opened. Dr. Flamand walked in, pushing a gurney with a body on it, draped in a bloody sheet. Natalie followed. Her hair was up, she was dressed exquisitely in blue satin brocade, and she was wearing Louise's face. She wasn't smiling, though her eyes were bright and lively. Flamand's work was too rough for her to have much use of the musculature around her mouth. The Doctor would have performed the operation flawlessly.

"Butcher," Louise said because he was.

He stopped and turned to face her, crouched there in her corner like some small, wounded animal. "I will assume it is only the pain talking, *chérie*. Not to worry. You are one of the immortals. One of the chosen. The skin will grow back, and then we can harvest you again—as many times as my poor Natalie needs." His smile was mad with lust and promise, but it was not like the Doctor's wicked smile. For the Doctor, that smile was all darkness and passion and hard-won knowledge. It belonged to him. With Andre Flamand, it was the smile of a conceited brat.

She hated that smile. She hated him. She was eaten through with her hatred of him. She launched herself at him, hands turned to killing claws, but Natalie stepped in and grabbed her by the throat like some pathetic rag doll, throwing her down.

"Behave, sister," Natalie said. "I told you. I'm much stronger than I look. And, after all, you don't want to become like Cherry." She un-sheeted the body. The faceless girl beneath was quite dead. Her body had been used and shorn apart. Little left could be called human.

Louise watched Natalie feed it through the teeth of the furnace while her brother crouched down beside her. He grabbed her by the raw meat of her face. He sank his spindly fingers into her wound. She had no more voice to scream. She simply showed her teeth, because that was what she was to him. An animal. A rabid lab animal.

"You are ours, Poppet," Flamand said, his voice scorching her fleshless face. "You belong to us. You are our creature now."

* * *

He finished packing his black medics bag and bundled himself in his long traveling coat. He pulled the collar up and pulled a hat down low over his bandaged face. This was like every other time he had gone out among his patients to perform a house call, but Rachel knew better.

She hovered uncertainly at the door. "Do you think she's all right? She is all right, isn't she?"

The Doctor reached out and touched her face. The moment he did, Rachel knew it would be all right. It was in his touch. In his doing. Dr. Faust could do anything.

"I will see to it," he told her. Moments later, he swept past her and down the tunnels that led up to the bowels of the well-gutted church. Above, one of his many agents in the city waited with a black car to take him seamlessly to the place of reckonings.

***

She was exquisite, a dream. Andre pinned Natalie to her sumptuous sleigh bed and thrust up and up into her tight velvet heaven until she cried out his name and clutched at him. When they both had come, he lowered his head and brushed her cheek with his hand, kissed the delicate rosebud of her lips. Her flesh was cooler than he liked, and he could taste an echo of decay even now, but, for the moment, she was perfect and whole and his.

"Brother," Natalie rasped, her eyelashes brushing the bruised plains of her cheeks. "Am I beautiful?"

"You are always beautiful," he lied, leaning down to tenderly kiss the bridge of her nose. The flesh moved slightly beneath his tongue and lips, but he didn't make mention of it. The Doctor's Poppet was so exquisite he hardly cared. She was a gorgeous fuckthing out of some dark dream. How did Faust not tear her to rags in this passion?

"You're looking at her," Natalie simpered.

"But I see only you. Shall I take you driving into the city, *chérie*?"

Natalie brightened immediately. Before the accident, she had been a beautiful little thing, always dancing for their father, always teasing Andre into her bed, but she hadn't possessed even the sense of a goose. In a hundred years, this had not changed. "Oh yes, yes, please."

He was prepared to lose himself inside of her one last time when he heard someone knock on the front door. Natalie looked up at him. Andre felt his anger razor keenly up his back. They had so little time before Natalie's body rejected the graft, and now this…yet more intruders! Standing up, he fixed his clothing and reached for the scalpel in his pocket. He would let the unfortunate soul in, hamstring him, and then let his pet do the rest.

He was halfway down the stairs to the foyer when the front doors were torn efficiently from their hinges and cast aside. Seconds later, his old adversary Dr. Faust entered the castle. He moved smoothly and economically, without hurrying. He was taller than Andre remembered, and dressed in all black. The house suddenly seemed colder for his arrival.

They eyed each other a long, keen moment.

"Faust," Andre hissed.

"You insufferable little brat," Faust answered.

Foul thing. Andre wanted to claw and rend at the creature before him, but he hesitated. There were stories told in the city. Perhaps they were made up. Perhaps not. But Natalie, standing beside him in only her shift, had not heard of them. Andre had kept them from her, as he had kept most unpleasantries from her, and she did the unthinkable. She grabbed the scalpel from his fingers and charged the Doctor with a scream.

"Natalie…!" Andre snatched at her but snagged only her gown. She was too quick to lunge and too powerful to hold back. The satin of the gown rent in his hand…

The Doctor caught Natalie at the wrists, halting her momentum. He lifted her high. She hissed and spat. Even in her best moments, she was feral. The accident had done more than ruin her face. It had scorched her mind. All this that Andre had done for her had been for the love of her, but it had been her idea ultimately. Without her, he would not have had the initiative—indeed, even the courage—to do any of it. But now she was in Faust's hands.

Faust glanced into her face. He saw.

Andre heard a sound in his throat like a train just before it wrecks. His body trembled with a kind of orgasmic rage. Turning, Faust smashed Natalie like an insect against the wall. Her neck snapped and the back of her head crackled like a bloody egg. She slumped down, leaving a snail's trail of blood and brain matter on the wainscoted wall, and the edges of her Louise face curled at the sutures. But her eyes saw. Her eyes were alive and moving in her wrecked body.

Andre stumbled backward up the stairs. Without Natalie, he was not a strong man. He was nothing. Faust made no sound as he followed, chuffing steadily forward like some demonic engine. "You brought this upon yourself, Faust! You did this!" Andre screamed, and when that didn't stop the encroaching darkness, he pointed. "It was she! It was Natalie! She's the monster, not me!"

Faust stopped. Andre thought—even prayed—that his old adversary would turn and take his terrible vengeance out on Natalie. That, at least, would give him a chance to escape intact...but it wasn't his words that had stopped the creature. Faust looked aside at a flight of stairs spiraling downward. The immortals were highly sensitive creatures. The Elixir made every sensation sing. He quickly picked up on the antiseptic scent of Andre's lab. It drew upon him. He turned and shushed shadow-like down the stairs, still carrying his bag.

Not that. Not the lab. The Poppet was his to use. His to have.

"Faust!" Andre screamed from the top of the stairs. *"Faust! Goddamn you!"*

Andre Flamand's voice bellowed up and up as the Doctor descended. Finally, he reached the lab and pushed through the swinging doors. A whimpering emanated from a room at the back—small, almost child-like. Broken.

The incinerator. The disposal room. It was there, at last, that Faust was reunited with his wife.

***

"Louise."

She clutched her corner and refused to look up at him. If she looked up, he would see. And then he would hate her. Or pity her, at the very least. Somehow, that was worse than anything.

"Louise."

"No, Doctor," she said, her voice coming muffled against the wall. "Don't look."

"I want to look." He wouldn't be dissuaded. That had never been his way. In the voice of her maker, he said, "Poppet, look at me."

She couldn't resist that command. Despite everything, she was still his creature. She lifted her head and looked up at him through the bloodied curtain of her hair.

He sank to one knee. He reached out and cupped her chin. He urged her chin up so he could better see the ruin of her face. His eyes flared.

"Doctor..." she said in a panic.

"Poppet," he answered, "you are the most beautiful woman in the world."

The burden on her heart lifted. She cried at the light of love in his eyes even as he guided her into his arms and laid his lips upon hers. He clutched the back of her head. He kissed her like that first time as if he couldn't get enough of her. Her taste. The feel of her.

His kiss hurt, but she didn't mind the pain. He was hers. He was her past and her future. He was the world, Above and Below.

"Oh, Doctor." She threw herself at him, clutched him like a prayer. She could feel his desire pressing into her, solid and true. He held her easily and she kissed him until his bandages were red with her blood. He licked her lips, gently and sensuously, and then kissed her one final time before letting her go and turning to the black medic's bag he had brought. From it, he withdrew his favorite scalpel and offered it to her.

He commanded her with no words. "Yes, Doctor," she said, taking it.

The time for pain and defeat was over. Now it was time to hunt their enemies.

***

Andre Flamand was standing at the front door, holding his sister in his arms, when they arrived. His face was contorted with bestial rage. His suit was coated in his sister's brain matter. "Get out of my house. Get out!" he bellowed at them both. His voice sounded rough and low, like a man possessed, a man enduring an orgasm of pain.

"No," Louise said evenly. She stood beside the Doctor, shoulder to shoulder with her husband. "I want my face back."

"You, *chérie*, can go straight to hell!"

"And," Louise bit the point of the scalpel, "I want your face."

Something bellowed in the depths of the House of Stairs. Flamand laughed knowingly before ducking out the door.

The Doctor turned just in time to face it head on as it collided with him, driving him to the floor under its brute black weight. It was a huge, befurred mountain of a creature. Its body was like that of a bear, but its two opposing heads looked human, and its arms strangely catlike, with big, beclawed paws at the end. It had a reptile's tail, and its feet were hoof-like, horse-like. In another place, Louise might have admired the work and obvious creativity that had gone into the chimera's creation, but this was Flamand's work. As a result, it was awkward, sophomoric, and badly sutured together. It looked like some big toy with badly fitted parts. Its eyes rolled crazily in its demented heads as it roared and beat at the Doctor, trying to crush him under repeated hammer blows to the chest.

She heard the puff of air that went out of the Doctor's lungs with each impact. She didn't think; she only reacted. She slashed deftly at the creature's hamstrings. That put it nicely off balance. The Doctor hissed a curse and raised his hand, his scalpel at the ready, but the creature was quicker than either of them had anticipated. It grabbed his arm and snapped it backward at the elbow. The Doctor grunted but that was all the sound he made. She seldom heard anything very loud or overexcited come from his mouth. The only time she could remember him raising his voice above a scorched whisper was when he was calling her to attention.

It lowered its lumbering body and its human heads bit at him. It was hurting him. It was hurting her Doctor, her master. Louise lunged at the creature with her blade, but it half-turned, backhanding her away. She fell the length of the foyer and into a doorway, stunned by the blow. Something was broken. She could sit up, but her legs were too mangled to stand.

The chimera was screaming unintelligible words into the Doctor's face. It scrabbled at him like a crazed animal. The Doctor did the only thing he could. With a grunt of labor, he drove his good arm up to the elbow in its chest cavity. The body, despite its great size, was soft and badly sewn together. It gave easily under his tremendous punch. The creature looked startled…then relieved. A human light came into its two sets of eyes. Finally, it articulated itself. "Yes..." one of the heads growled out in fetid breath. "Yes, kill, kill..." said the other.

The Doctor jerked his arm out, holding its black jelly heart in his hand. With a hiss of determination, he drove his arm back into the cavity, dragging out more quivering inner things, some of which did not seem to belong to any of the creatures the chimera was comprised of. Stinking black blood bathed him up and down, flecking his white bandages, making his coat shine like satin, but he did not stop. Rather, he worked slowly and efficiently, ransacking the creature while it trembled and danced. Eventually, it fell still and empty upon him, a husk. He thrust the creature away and stood up, his arm hanging brokenly at his side.

"Doctor..." she said as he wrenched his arm back into place and moved to aid her.

"Let me fix you." He shifted the bones in her legs until she felt a dull spike of pain up her back. Slowly, her body began returning to prickly life. "And now..." he said, taking her hand and guiding her to her feet.

"Yes," she answered and gripped the knife yet tighter.

***

Flamand was loading Natalie into his car when Louise caught up to him. He looked surprised to see she had escaped the house relatively unscathed.

She moved with predatory grace, not frantically but efficiently—the way the Doctor had taught her. She raised her hand, the scalpel in it. Flamand turned to deflect her blade, to protect his sister, but she had anticipated his move. She turned with an economy of motion and swung the petite blade in a wide, low arc. The first cut caught him high up on the thigh. The Doctor's knives were kept as sharp as broken glass. They were able to penetrate layers of meat and muscle in a single stroke. She cut him to the bone, the blade sparking against his femur.

He went down with a cry like some wounded dove, but she did not stop there. As he folded to his knees, she cut him again, then again. Each cut penetrated to the bone, separating the epidermis and muscle tissue with no trouble at all. Each cut made him cry out and twist. He tried to grab at her, to defend himself, but she was faster than he, and angrier. She made her cuts quickly and decisively until he was a quivering lump lying on the gravel, surrounded by the black juice of his own unnatural inner workings.

"I only did it for her. For the love of her." Flamand hid his face, convinced she would take it.

But she didn't want that. The Doctor had taught her well. Physical pain was brief and fleeting. It was the pain of the eternal soul. Timeless. It changed you. It made you better. And worse.

She grabbed Natalie by the hair and threw her easily over one shoulder. She shrieked like a machine as they made their way back toward the house, but there was little she could do with her neck broken the way it was. It would take too long to heal, and they were descending into the depths of the house too quickly. It wasn't difficult for Louise to drag Natalie Flamand through the twisted warren of hallways and down the mad staircases to the lab below. Soon they were alone in that dismal little disposal room.

There, Natalie promised her anything if she would only let her go. She promised Louise money. She promised to leave the city and never return. She pleaded with Louise to think of love, to let her go back to her brother who was her whole world. Louise forced the begging, hysterical creature with her stolen face into the furnace, half expecting her dear brother to try one last valiant rescue. But Flamand was no prince—indeed, no decent monster—and he never showed.

***

She heard a voice calling to her on her way out of the house. She followed it up and down the many staircases until she reached an upstairs bedroom. There Louise pushed the door open.

Jacob was roped to the headboard of a huge, pillared bed. He looked beaten and bruised, but he lived. She was surprised to see him here. As she approached the bed, he began to fight and scream.

Her face. Of course.

She stopped at his bedside and looked down at him. He was terrified of her, that much was obvious, but pain and trauma at the hands of the Flamands had fortified him, and, after a moment, he seemed more afraid for his daughter's wellbeing than his own safety.

"Gio...please, Louise, Gio...she's in the car. She's probably scared to death."

"Yes, Jacob."

"Louise...get Gio. Get Gio, please! Keep her safe."

"I understand," she answered. Her face itched as it struggled to heal and she wanted to scratch it. But she wanted to talk to Jacob more. "I'll protect her. I'll be her mother."

"Wait...no...Louise? What are you talking about? Louise...!"

Her hand flickered out. With a single, decisive gesture, Jacob's throat was cut. His body pulsed out great rivers of red onto the bedclothes and pillow. He watched her with a comical mixture of bemusement and disbelief, but she didn't think he suffered. There was no pain upon his face, and that pleased her immensely. Jacob was her friend; he didn't deserve to suffer.

Jacob hadn't known her. He had been inside her, but he had never been within her, not as the Doctor was. She waited until he was finished, until he was empty of life, then went downstairs to the car, Natalie's small white dog following her, and removed the sleeping Gio from her car seat.

"M-a...a?" Gio inquired sleepily.

"Yes, I'm here," Louise told the little girl in her arms. She held her close against the shelter of her body. "Mother is here."

The Doctor stood stoically nearby, watching them. Andre Flamand was nowhere to be found, and his car was gone. She wasn't at all surprised by that. In the end, his love for his sister was nothing compared to her love for the Doctor. It was all. It was the world.

When she turned to face her husband, she found a smile peeling back the edges of her raw red lips. "Now," she said, taking the Doctor's hand, "*now* we can be a family."

FOR THE ONE I LOVE: A DOCTOR FAUST STORY

| 20 |

February 14, 20--

Growing up, I'd never had much use for Valentine's Day.
It was always so cold and white and blue. A sea of ice separating every living thing from the salvation of spring. The day was spent eating bitter little candy hearts and trading Snoopy and Disney Princess paper valentines with students I didn't like and who didn't like me. But we were told by our teachers to be polite and to give everyone a valentine, which didn't make any sense to me. I'd always thought that valentines were supposed to mean something. What did it mean to give someone you didn't like a paper cartoon heart?

I didn't like the movies they played on TV or the power ballads they played on the radio. None of it was real. It was all fabricated digital flesh and clever wordplay. I had never known anyone to fall in love at first sight. The first time I'd looked upon the Doctor, I'd been scared. I was sure he would kill me. Sometimes—but not often—I still wished he had.

This one time, I found Valentine's Day cards in a manila folder in the attic of the old clapboard farmhouse where I grew up. I wasn't looking for them. I was looking for Daddy's diploma. A girl at school said he couldn't read or write, that he was trash. That I was, too. I'd wanted to prove her wrong, so I crept up the narrow wooden stairs after Daddy had gone to bed to look for his diploma. I knew if I showed it to the girl who had called him trash, she would have to take it back. If she didn't, I would hit her in the mouth or something.

But I didn't find the diploma. I found the cards, instead. They were to Momma from Daddy. They were pretty, sparkly red and white, full of naked winged babies, but all marked up because Daddy had scrawled bad words all over them. I knew then that the girl was wrong. Daddy could read and write. But then Daddy caught me looking at the cards. I guess the bouncy old floorboards had given me away.

"Give me those and get your skinny ass downstairs!" he barked at me. "You go to bed right now!"

I fled down the stairs, almost tripping on the last step. I didn't want to get hit, even though Daddy had stopped doing that long ago. As I dashed through the open attic door, I heard him shout, "You're as bad as her! You're both shits!"

His anger sickened me like an old, familiar snake tightening up in my stomach. Venom makes you cold, I'd read once. It freezes your blood. So I'd never really liked Valentine's Day. I'd thought of it as one of the Bad Days, like Christmas, and my birthday. Days when Daddy meant well but got drunk and angry and snapped like a snake.

Yet the moment I woke up this morning, I knew something was different, something was special about the day. Last year, on this day, the Doctor and I were too busy to celebrate. One of the girls we both knew had fallen on the ice. She was one of the People of the Tunnels, and she had also been pregnant. She had torn her uterus in the fall. Or, rather, it had prolapsed, as the Doctor had patiently explained to me as he worked. It was a fairly complicated surgery, and it had taken us most of the afternoon to tend to her.

That evening, in the quiet, familiar stuffiness of the study, we took tea and the Doctor said to me, "I ruined your day, Poppet. I wanted to give you something special."

"It was her day," I explained while Rachel served us tea and cucumber sandwiches, a favorite of mine. I did not tell him that I didn't like this holiday. There were times when we spoke at length about my past, but how could my adventures compare to his? He had seen and written pieces of history. I felt mundane and tiring, so I often kept things to myself. Besides, I kept thinking about the child inside the girl, the child we had saved. We had done a good thing today. The Doctor called it balancing the scales.

"And," I added, "you already give me things." Just the other day, he had given me a book of paleontology with a fossilized trilobite as a bookmark.

"Something unique," he amended his statement. "Something befitting Persephone herself." He sat very still as he usually did, like he wasn't a real thing, all unbreathing darkness and fire-lit shadows, and watched me through the bandages. They were dark after so many hours of work. He was bleeding through. I was bleeding with him, not through my face, but my heart.

I could feel his fatigue. His longing. It was as sharp inside of me as one of his instruments.

I slipped to the floor at his feet and laid my head in his lap. He touched my hair. His touch was gentle and playful, though I knew he could have wrenched my skull to puzzle pieces, if that was his desire. "If you are willing to be patient, my dear, I shall give it to you soon."

I didn't know what he could give me that he hadn't already, but I nodded all the same. At the time, I'd been almost insatiably curious, but after a while, I thought maybe he had forgotten, or that what he had wanted to give me was too difficult to find. But he could get anything. Cosmetics from Cairo, and dresses from the Dominican

Republic. The vintage combs and mourning jewelry he gave me were from auctions in places I had never heard of before. But he knew how to find them all.

Eventually, things had come to pass with Lizabeth and with Dr. Flamand—and all those lovely, sad things with Jacob—and I forgot even more. I had duties now. I had a child to see after. Charlotte. And a mother's work is never done.

Her name hadn't been that when she came to me, but it was what we called her. Since the Doctor's treatment, she could remember little of her life before. I was much the same way. I remembered some things, of course, like the valentines in the attic, but they were archaic occurrences that belonged to distant times. Every year they faded a little more around the edges. I knew Charlotte felt the same.

She is four now, but like all the Timeless, she is as ageless as stone and sky. She is very small and slight and needs to be carried. I don't mind carrying her. I carry her everywhere she wants to go. She likes it when the Doctor carries her. He is very tall and she gets to almost touch the ceiling.

"Momma up," she used to say to me, but she's become wonderfully articulate now. "Momma, I want to go up" is her favorite expression. That and "Doc-doc, take me up." Soon, we will teach her all kinds of languages, and she will learn about medicine and math. I was very good at math in school.

"Momma, no more crib," Charlotte said when I stepped into the nursery this morning. She was standing up in her little white nightshift and bonnet and eyeing me with her clever grey eyes. "I want a bed."

"You'll fall out of bed," I said, picking her up.

She squirmed. "Down." She pointed at the floor. "Not a doll."

I put her down but held her hand as I led her to the changing screen.

"Want a bed!" she insisted while I dressed her for the day in a dress and pinafore, socks and shoes, which she tied up herself.

"You don't sleep in a crib," she complained while I wrestled with her curls in the vanity mirror. I put in a ribbon and she pulled it loose and threw it aside. "Doctor doesn't sleep in a crib."

This was the first time she was addressing him properly. "Of course he doesn't," I said. "He is the Doctor."

"No ribbons. No cribs!"

"Very well. I'll speak to the Doctor about it," I told her as a pleasant, plain-faced Rachel appeared in the doorway of the nursery to take Charlotte into the library for her lessons for the day.

"Fetch me if she's difficult," I told Rachel.

"She's never difficult," Rachel insisted. She was very good at looking after Charlotte. She was leading her own child Matthew by the hand and I knew he and Charlotte would spend many hours reading to each other under the somber lights of the candelabras while some rambling Tchaikovsky played in the background. This was their day. Books and music. Charlotte was learning from the ground up as I had.

I returned to my bedchamber. The Doctor had long since gone. A mission into the city for supplies, he had said. But this morning, as every morning before, he had left his choice of dress at the foot of the antique sleigh bed we shared. It was sharp-edged taffeta, light as air, and red as an open heart. I lifted the fabric to my face. It smelled of history and newness in equal measure. Modern haute couture and antiquated design.

Beneath it lay a yellow envelope, sealed with red candle wax.

This, too, I lifted up, then turned to the altar of candles opposite the bed to better read the fine white parchment within. Five words were scrawled on it in the Doctor's cramped, delicate calligraphy: *For the One I Love.*

Accompanying it were a pair of tickets to see Sarah Brightman at a one-night-only, closed performance at the Chelsea Opera. I had heard of it. I had longed for it, as well. Perhaps I had said something at tea. I couldn't recall. Or he knew. The Doctor always knew. Regardless, it was such a private affair that only a hundred VIPs were invited.

Unsurprisingly, the Doctor was among the elite. And *noblesse oblige* required we attend.

* * *

The limousine coasted to a stop in the curb and the driver came around to hold the door for us. The Doctor did something very unusual then. He stepped out onto the walk beneath the sterile glow of a streetlamp before reaching down to guide me from the vehicle. "You look lovely tonight," he told me, his voice modulated to affect a rich but airy tone that revealed nothing unpleasant.

I had seen him out in society only twice before. The first time was when he had come for me at Dr. Flamand's mansion, and the second time was a few weeks ago when we had attended a performance of *La Boheme* at the Metropolitan Opera. The first time—at the House of Stairs—he had worn his bandages. The second time we had had a seasonal box, though he had not sat with me. I wasn't sure where he had gone, but I had found the performance dulled by his lack of presence. I had wanted to discuss the story with him, but he had chosen to watch from some other more private vantage point. I had been tempted to argue, but he had good reason not to make public appearances.

Tonight was different. I could not stop looking at him. A spare black shadow in an evening dress and a cravat like a red open wound at his throat.

His flesh mechanics were immaculate. Spectral. I could find no seam in his face, no stitch in his fine, cream-white skin. He looked as I imagined he had as that young, willful surgeon in the workhouse in 1878, pure and untouched by the world's atrocities. But then, this had always been in him. He had his work, his body farm. There was no reason to be so surprised.

I thought of his excuse. Fetching supplies—which he never did. He had agents for the more mundane tasks. He had not wanted me to know. He hadn't wanted me frightened by his hours of careful labor. The pain that had surely been unendurable. I thought of it now—every searing suture, every troublesome knot that aggravated and enflamed his bleeding meat. I embraced those imagined agonies and held them inside of me like a little flame on a cold blue Valentine's night.

He did not smile, but that was to be expected. His mimetic muscle had been brutally scraped away, and what little remained had long since atrophied. Smiling would only ruin the illusion.

"Not just I," I admitted as I joined him on the sidewalk. I could not look away from him. He was the black hole around which the earth rotated. He was my gravity. And when he tucked my hand into the crook of his arm, I felt I belonged more to him in that moment than in all the nights we had spent together. We were a couple. We were a we. Like the dozens of others moving in ordered circles about the city. Invisible, and yet small pieces of it.

I had never felt the sharp, sterile edges of love until this moment. While we moved inside the gilded, vault-like structure, I kept my eyes on him. The coolness of his arm seeped into my hand, reminding me of what he was. What we were together. We would be this thing in a year, a century, a millennium. Each sluggish tick of my pulse seemed to seek its counterpart in him.

My voice was unaccountably shy as if we were meeting for the first time. "Tear my heart out," I told him. "It only beats when you hold it, Doctor."

"My dear," he said, and that was all.

The ushers seated us in a special box overlooking the stage. There were lovely little mother-of-pearl opera glasses presented to me in an engraved leather case, more a memento than a necessity, and shortly before the performance, another of the Doctor's agents presented me with a traditional bouquet of roses dipped in 24-carat gold.

I had never dreamed of receiving such fine gifts. I had only read about such things. I fingered the roses with delicate interest while we waited for the curtain to rise. They were another of the Doctor's creations. The stems had been constructed of delicate little bones sewn all together, and the heads were large and frilly, the plated petals meticulously molded from out of the Doctor's body farm.

The little note said in whispering gold gilt: *For the One I Love.*

"All of this is quite too much," I chastised him. I made my voice sweet and shy, the way he liked it. "Your gifts have spoiled me, Doctor."

"These are merely a prelude," he told me, taking my hand in his as the lights went down. "You'll receive your gift later on, Poppet."

Another gift! I felt a quiver of anticipation.

The performance was sublime, of course. Ms. Brightman seemed to be singing to each of us in particular—but, then, I think everyone in attendance felt that way. The music became a living thing, quavering but painfully breakable, a barrier against the real world lurking outside the doors of the opera house. For a little while we were entombed.

After the ovation, the Doctor's hand closed incrementally tighter about my hand and he lifted it to his delicately constructed lips to kiss. "And now."

"Really. You mustn't spoil me."

"It is a husband's prerogative to spoil his wife on such a night," he answered and lifted me from my seat. "Tonight is your night, my dear. It has been constructed for your pleasure."

The cold, crisp night struck us like a slap. Though the limousine waited at the curb, I asked to stand in the night with the Doctor. I wanted to feel a part of the city. I wanted to watch the other Valentine's Day couples rushing to their appointments.

In my mind, I saw myself taking his hand and coasting across the busy street, disappearing into the fray of lights like a pair of rangy teenage lovers. We might see the art of Battery Park, or go for a ride in a horse-drawn carriage down the cobblestones of Central Park West. In movies, lovers visited the Observation Deck of the Empire State Building and whispered lifelong ambitions in each other's ears. But I suppose we were not that kind of couple. Though his face remained patiently flawless, I could see the ghost of pain in it. He was hurting for his love of me. The scratch and tick of nerve endings pulled too taut and fastened too stiffly in place. Tonight was slowly coming undone, all the masks coming off.

I lifted his hand to my cheek and closed my eyes and said, "Yes. Now."

* * *

The restaurant he had chosen to close out this evening was located in the East Village. In all honesty, it was not someplace I would have chosen to dine. I recognized it as soon as we turned onto the avenue, and slowly, bit by bit, as we approached, I felt a muscle in my belly twitch and tighten until it seemed my body was being grossly yanked inside out by my old familiar friend the snake.

I had been here once before, a long time ago. I remembered the fetid alley with its rusting Dumpster and graffiti-darkened walls. The light that never seemed to penetrate the dark places. The sweet smell of decay and blackened grease hung on the air.

When I was fifteen, I left that old farmhouse with the haunted valentines in the attic. I wore a hoodie and carried my gym duffel. My pockets were full of money I'd taken from Daddy's wallet. The night before, Daddy had made me bleed. That wasn't unusual in and of itself, but during volleyball in gym class the following day, the blood had started again, and one of the girls had laughed and thrown me a tampon. I'd laughed with her and we had shared one of those wordless moments between women besieged by their own traitorous bodies, but she didn't know the truth. No one did. What was the point of telling? No one ever believed you, or they thought you were looking for attention, or that you were crazy or just bad. Sometimes they put you on medication, and I didn't want to be doped up one night when I had to get out of the house real fast.

The bus let me off at Port Authority in the East Village. The vertigo of people rushing back and forth made me so dizzy, that I almost couldn't stand up. I sat down for a while in a chair near the bathrooms and must have fallen asleep. When I woke up, my duffel was gone, and even my hoodie's pockets had been torn out. I was hungry. I wanted to go home, but I didn't even have the money for a ticket.

I wandered around for a long time. I kept thinking I would get an idea, but nothing came to me. I was alone. I might as well be an alien in a strange land where no one wanted me.

When all the lights started coming on and I realized it was getting dark, which never really happens here, I knew I was in trouble. I needed to sleep. But more than that, I needed to eat. I hadn't eaten in at least a day. Everything was surreal, and I wanted to cry, but I was afraid to because I thought for sure they would know I wasn't from this place, and then they would come for me. They would smell my fear and make me pay.

The ambient scents of a distant restaurant attracted me. It was like carrion to vultures, and I thought about that sometime later while I dug through a bin at the back. There was a lot of really good food being thrown out! I was stuffing my pockets for later when the owner threw open a heavy door marked with a Private sign and started yelling at me. "Get away from there, you little shit! What do you think you're doing?"

She was a large, solid woman. She should have been pretty, but her face was all hard planes full of so much anger that I thought I should see cracks around her mouth and eyes. She was dressed smartly, and diamonds crackled at her throat and on her fingers. I was surprised when she came at me. I didn't understand why she should be so mad at me. I wasn't disturbing her establishment. I wasn't making a sound.

She grabbed my hair unexpectedly and spun me around. "You pieces of shit never learn, do you?" She said it like this had been going on for a long time. I thought maybe I could reason with her. I had seen girls on the run on TV do that. They were given storerooms to sleep in and slowly made their way up the ranks of the city. They became someone. I hoped to be that girl. But she shook me, then ripped at my hoodie. All my food fell out. Then she slapped me smartly across the face.

I let her do it. I don't know why. I guess I didn't think she would do those things. I never thought Daddy would until he did them.

When she pushed me backward, I stumbled and fell. I was usually very balanced on my feet. Light as a bird. I used to dance ballet when I was little. But I was also tired and hungry and my body felt like bags of concrete sewn together. I fell hard with a yelp. She raised her fist above her head like she would smash me. I scrambled up, turned, and hit the Dumpster crouched behind me. I hit hard and a flower of pain bloomed across my nose and cheeks.

The woman laughed at that. She laughed at how badly I had hurt myself. How much she had frightened me.

I knew, then, that I wasn't one of those TV girls. They weren't real. Only this was real, this despair swallowing my stomach with snake-like accuracy. This cold, blue humiliation in the February streets.

I picked myself up a little more carefully. There was blood peppering my hands and hair. I was so dizzy I wanted to heave, but I managed to run away, too surprised by everything to even feel the pain surging through my face. That came later after I found a place to sleep under a bridge down by the river where a lot of the street people gathered about their burn barrels and bonfires.

"Doctor..." I said now, putting a hand on his arm.

"Yes, Poppet," he answered. His hand hovered in the air in front of his face as if to staunch the flow of his unseen agony.

I felt ashamed of my reaction. He had obviously invested much in this evening. His time, his art, and his suffering. Though I was certain I must have recounted my story about the alley, perhaps he had forgotten it or misinterpreted it in some way. Or perhaps this was a test of some kind. I would not fail him. I would swallow my insides coming out. I would be the proper lady he knew me to be.

I said, "I...thank you for this evening."

"It's hardly over," he said, lowering his hand and placing it upon mine. His fingers were cold like artificial skin stretched over bones of cleverly constructed steel. His enormous strength seemed to enter me through his touch.

He walked me inside, a place I had never been before. I immediately recognized the maitre d' as one of the Doctor's most trusted agents. That confused me until I spotted one of the wait staff. I recognized her, as well.

I stopped in the middle of the floor. We were starkly alone in the arctic whiteness of an enormously posh dining room. It might have seemed vast, were the lights on, but it was dark except for a table at the center of the floor where a bowl of floating candles threw forth a mask of sallow yellow light. Despite the carefully constructed elegance, I found the place sad and rather ugly.

"You have been wonderfully patient about your gift, Poppet," the Doctor said. He led me toward the table set with a white linen tablecloth and a centerpiece of white and yellow calla lilies, their tongues lolling toward the ribbed ceiling. The table was set with fine crystal dinnerware and gold-plated cutlery, but, curiously enough, there were three places set for dinner.

The Doctor seated me first, then himself. One of his agents stepped up beside him and the Doctor turned his head and nodded to him. "Please."

I waited, my heart thudding up around my throat. As Timeless, our meals are decorative rather than functional, but that doesn't mean we enjoy them any less. Eating itself had become our art, something we shared and improved upon.

More agents emerged from the kitchen. They were ushering forth the woman from the alley, the one who had laughed at me. She moved languidly, with almost clockwork precision, her eyes unfocused on her environment. From experience, I knew she was heavily sedated.

"Doctor," I said. My voice was surprisingly distressed. I touched my face where a ghostly flare of pain seemed to dwell.

"Sit down," he told me. "Be still, Poppet."

It took me a moment to realize I was on my feet. He stood and touched the back of my chair. "Sit," he said once more, using the gravity of his voice to bind me.

Sitting there, his guest and prisoner, I lowered my head. There was a card on my plate that had gone unnoticed by me until now.

For the One I Love.

I looked up. Our agents were lowering the woman into the third seat. She lolled drunkenly, but when her gaze drifted toward me, I could see something. Through the haze of medication, something had clicked in her mind. Some familiarity. My face was different. Timeless. Yet she recognized me. She bared her teeth like a mad horse. "...ittle shhhhit!" she spat at me. She shoved at the table defiantly, dislodging her plate and silverware.

"Vile woman," the Doctor said. His voice was calm and persuasive. "You will learn your manners."

She slurred a series of curses at the Doctor. She called him the devil, and I the devil's whore.

"Be silent," he said, and, much to my surprise, she did as he bade her, though she weaved dangerously in her seat.

He turned to me. "Do you approve of my new formula?"

How curious. "What does it do, Doctor?"

"Whatever you want." He paused thoughtfully. "Whatever you command, Poppet."

My gift. Oh, the Doctor was much too good to me! No paper valentines or bitter candy hearts. No black skies or blue moons. The Doctor, more than anyone, knew that Valentine's Day was hot and red and full of insouciant life. More than anyone, he knows how well it bleeds and squirms, like the endless screaming of dogged, stubborn life.

He, more than anyone, understands me. The one I love.

I considered all the possibilities before giving the woman her first command.

"No," she begged and begged again. Her anger had left her. Perhaps the snake in her stomach had eaten it all up. But the Doctor's potions were strong. There was no escaping his wizardry.

She had some difficulty working the cutlery through the tough muscle of her upper thigh. The femoral muscles are some of the most widely used in the human body. "Fuck you," she hissed, sweating through the pain as she transferred the first quivering pieces of red meat to her plate. Her hands were under my control, but her mind wandered while I commanded her to cut her dinner into small pieces. We had a long night ahead of us, and I didn't want her to choke.

ABOUT THE AUTHOR

K.H. Koehler is the bestselling author of various novels and novellas in the genres of horror, SF, dark fantasy, steampunk, and young and new adult. She is the owner of KH Koehler Books and KH Koehler Design, which specializes in graphic design and professional copyediting. Her books are widely available at all major online distributors and her covers have appeared on numerous books in many different genres. Her short work has appeared in various anthologies, and her novel series include *The Kaiju Hunter*, *A Clockwork Vampire*, *Planet of Dinosaurs*, *The Nick Englebrecht Mysteries*, and *The Archaeologists*. She is the author of multiple Amazon bestsellers and was one of the founders and chief editors of KHP Publishers, which published genre fiction from 2001 to 2015. She has over fifteen years of experience in the publishing industry as a writer, ghostwriter, copyeditor, commercial book cover designer, formatter, and marketer. Visit her website at https://khkoehler.net.

www.ingramcontent.com/pod-product-compliance
Lightning Source LLC
LaVergne TN
LVHW030321070526
838199LV00069B/6517